D1528917

Goodbye, Friends

Goodbye, Friends

Stories

B.A. Phillips

Bridge Works Publishing Co.
Bridgehampton, New York

Library of Congress Cataloging-in-Publication Data

Phillips, B.A. (Barbara Ann).
Goodbye, friends: stories/B.A. Phillips
p. cm.
ISBN 1-882593-01-4 (acid-free paper)
I. Title.
PS3566.H4758G66   1993
813'.54—dc20   92-43030
CIP

10 9 8 7 6 5 4 3 2 1

"Are We Almost There?" appeared originally in a somewhat different form in the literary magazine *Ascent*, and "A Little Lovely Dream" in *The East Hampton* (N.Y.) *Star*.

Grateful acknowledgment is made to the following for permission to reprint song titles and/or lines:

Hampshire House Publishing Co., New York, N.Y., for "Fly Me To the Moon and Let Me Play Among the Stars," from "Fly Me To the Moon (In Other Words)." Words and Music by Bart Howard, *TRO-* Copyright © 1954 (renewed).

Warner/Chappell Music, Inc. for "Adios Muchachos, compañeros, de me vida" from "Adios Muchachos" (Julio Cesar Sanders).

Paul Simon Music, New York, N.Y. for six lines from "The 59th Street Bridge Song," copyright © 1966 Paul Simon.

EMI Music Publishing for one line from "Me and Bobby McGee" by Kris Kristofferson & Fred Foster, copyright © 1969 *Temi Combine Inc.* All rights controlled by *Combine Music Corp.* Administered by *EMI Blackwood Music Inc.*

Stay Straight Music for six lines from "Long Time Gone," words and music by David Crosby, copyright © 1968.

CPP/Belwin, Inc. P.O. Box 4340, Miami, FL 33014, for one line from "Hernando's Hideaway" by Richard Adler & Jerry Ross, copyright © 1954 *Frank Music Corp.* Renewed 1982 *Richard Adler Music* and *J & J Ross Company* c/o The Songwriters Guild. International Copyright Secured. Made in USA. All rights reserved.

Book jacket art by Vikki Nicolson, in the collection of the author
Book and jacket design by Edith Allard

Printed in the United States of America

First Edition

To the gang at Ashawagh Hall,
and to Erika,
with affection and gratitude

Contents

Goodbye, Friends

Getting the Blues

❀ ——————————————— ❀

*I*n an hour the beach will be dark. Surf casters in down jackets and shoulder-high waders arrange themselves like totems on the shelf of the pounding October surf. Their 4×4s squat on the dunes behind, bristling rods like cheerleaders at a sporting event. Up and down the tide line Labs and Goldens, crazed by the outing and the smell of rot, bark and leap at seagulls wheeling just out of reach. Bluefish are running.

Mary Fodor shivers a little as the feeble sun departs, complaining to her companion, Hilda Simpson, "I'm not physical like you. I'll never get the hang of this." Hilda smiles encouragingly, but Mary knows her limitations. For the last six months, she has tried her hardest to please Hilda. She needs her friend's approval, needs the expansion that accompanies affection, as if she were a puny plant and Hilda a grow light. But in all her 37 years, Mary has never dealt with as difficult a problem as attempting to cast into the dark deep a length of nylon line crowned by a dangerous hook. Hilda has remarked many times that fishermen are God's chosen people, clever and coordinated. Indeed, up and down the beach, these anointed cry out like victorious warriors as they haul in variously sized blues. But Mary, even as a girl, could never throw a ball, and Hilda says that a good cast is like a good pitch, using the wrist and arm, with a deep follow-through.

Hilda, of course, is an experienced angler, with a calm competence that comes from years of practice. She understands the sport, knows its lore by heart. Each year about this time, she regularly scans the ocean when fish are migrating to southern waters, until she or another keen-eyed observer spots a telltale turbulence where schools of small fish are moving closer to shore and warmer water. These bait fish are pursued by their hungry fellows, the larger bluefish. Suddenly, as if informed by native drums, dozens of fishermen appear at once on a particular stretch of beach, ready for action.

Mary envies the skill with which her friend handles her rod and reel, like a chef with a frypan. She can send the monofilament line, the single strand nylon that in Mary's hands whips into tangles in the blink of an eye, out into the sea with a wrist flick that seems no more difficult than tossing flapjacks.

After all Hilda's coaching, Mary's movements are still clumsy, either too slow or too fast, and today she has yet to get a nibble. She imagines that the wide beach is beginning to rebuke her, that the other fishermen are watching her in pity. Shrilling gulls laugh at her clumsiness, cry at her that she will never be able to snap her wrist and follow through with her arm, sending the reel spinning and the line flying through the air, landing the lure with a gentle "plop" close to the voracious bluefish swimming just below the surface.

The harder Mary tries casting and retrieving, the colder and more frustrated she gets. But stubbornness prods her. Even if she is, as Hilda's children would describe it, a "spaz" at fishing, it is important that she keep at it. Hilda admires courage.

Besides, something positive is destined to emerge from this dreary exercise, despite Mary's feebleness and the seawater splashing into her too-short boots. She fixes the scene — pale sky, opaque sea, rapacious birds — firmly into her consciousness. Whether she catches a fish or splashes in the surf until she falls on her face with exhaustion, she will eventually come to describe the experience. Mary is a poet.

Before she met Hilda, intellectual pursuits had sustained her. For most of her adult years, Mary taught poetry composition to elder citizens in a series of apartments and community centers, for the pittances that supported her meager needs. In the evenings or on weekends, she read her own work in one or another bookstore or artist's loft to fellow followers of the muse. She and her literary friends polished their sonnets and short stories, published them in obscure literary magazines and sometimes, to greater acclaim and more money, in publications for the general reader. In the main, the members of the literary group gave each other moral support and general approbation, or endured with patience the occasional discouraging word. None was wealthy or successful, but they were splendidly indifferent to the concerns of the commercial philistines.

"Hold your left hand right at the bottom of the rod and use it as a guide," Hilda says to Mary. Early on, she had assured Mary that learning to fish was a snap, as simple as brushing your teeth.

Mary grits her perfectly shaped, white molars, one of

her most impressive features. For the tenth time, she throws out her rod and watches the line curl and sag into the nearest breaker. Her feeling of inadequacy is a new and dangerous emotion.

Covered from head to toe in rubber and down, Hilda pretends not to notice her friend's awkward casts. Her own arms resemble windmill paddles as she casts and reels, casts and reels. She has already caught three bluefish, now dying slowly in a bucket of seawater.

To help Mary relax, Hilda jokes with the local beach boys. She knows them all — the real estate salesman, the builder, the King Kullen manager — the guys whose Jeeps and Chevy vans bear bumper stickers reading "I'd Rather Be Fishing" and "Eat Fish, Live Longer; Eat Bass, Love Longer," the sporting maniacs who leave their loved ones to shore up the home front while they chase bluefish and bass, cobia and sea trout up and down the beaches and seas of the world. Hilda is comfortable being one of only two women fishing, but she knows that Mary would prefer to be invisible.

"Ned, you gotta take lessons if you wanna catch fish," Hilda calls, or "Lou, they were bitin' real good until you showed up." A couple of the fishermen are youngish and attractive. Their admiration for Hilda seems genuine; she's one of them, asking no favors, receiving none. They say to Mary, "Good teacher there. Simpson's no slouch."

Mary agrees. The night the two women met, she had been giving a reading at Tonio's, a bookstore in the little town north of the beach. As she was launching into "Sign of Shock," a plea for nuclear disarmament, she noticed a woman who wasn't a regular. The woman, six feet tall with frizzy blonde hair, wearing a thigh-high miniskirt and a tight angora sweater, had secured an illegal glass of wine before the readings. Drinks were only served at the end of each performance, to discourage any wavering of concentration during the feats of execution on display. To Mary, the woman was an anomaly in this environment, seemingly more at home at Caldor's searching out the latest Danielle Steel.

But the woman's fixed gaze, as if she planned to leap up and challenge Mary's credentials should her rhythm or imagery falter, made Mary pay special attention to her voice projection. Her recitation took on new drama and spirit. Strangely, she wanted this woman to approve of her, of her talent and ambitions.

After the reading, the blonde joined the congratulatory group around Mary. She towered over them, her head shaking like a giant dandelion, a second glass of wine slopping over as she spoke.

"My name is Hilda Simpson," she said, in a Chianti rush, grabbing Mary away from her fans. "And I lo-ove your poetry. Of course I prefer stuff that rhymes, because I compose music for a church choir. How about coming to dinner sometime? Read me some more of your stuff? I bet we could turn it into some terrific hymns."

That encounter, thinks Mary, was only six months ago. Then, she had been astonished and pleased; no one as lively as Hilda Simpson had ever taken an interest in her. In general, her friends were serious, driven, humorless. Hilda seemed to Mary like an explosive charge, prepared to demolish the old and drab, revealing instead the possibilities of new openness.

Now, she watches Hilda flick her wrist and toss her rod at the sea as if she means to throw her gear away. The curved arc of Hilda's cast, not so high that the line is deflected by the wind, but not so low that the lure plops into the breakers at her feet, swivels out toward the horizon and falls like a stone.

Some of the men are watching Hilda, too. "Shoot, you could walk on the blues out here today," says the old fellow to Mary's right. He has only caught one, himself. But Hilda doesn't take offense. With her eyes fixed on the water, she comments, "You tell 'em, Charley, and we're a lot more comfy than if we were rockin' and rollin' out there," gesturing toward the horizon where the rollers plane.

Not for the first time, Mary marvels at her friend's ease, her secure demeanor. Hilda is divorced, with two kids, no education to speak of and no marketable skills. She lives on a tiny alimony supplemented by selling fish and the raspberries she grows in her back garden. But she lunges at life exactly as a fighting fish lunges at a hook. She approaches every experience with the intensity of an Olympic hopeful. Hilda's favorite maxim is "You can't win if you're not at the table."

Mary is deafened by a scream in her ear. "Alll-right, a strike!" Hilda is reeling fast, her rod shimmying in protest. Something enormous is objecting to the fishhook. Hilda sticks the butt end of the rod between her thighs and secures her heavy rubber waders in the surf, an armored Juno.

The rod begins to bend dangerously — to Mary's eyes, ready to snap. Hilda, unconcerned, draws the rod upward, as if to snatch the fish from its home. But instead of reeling, she holds the drag steady, allowing the fish to take off again with the line. "Tirin' him out," she grins at Mary.

Mary thinks that Hilda has snagged her as skillfully as the struggling fish. That night at the bookstore, she had been dubious of the towheaded giantess. Mary's life was solitary, but predictable. A small trust fund gave her the independence to play out her verses in college bookstores and obscure literary magazines. Her parents in Florida had given up hope of a son-in-law or grandchildren, and presented to their fellow retirees, instead of baby pictures, each new sonnet that made its way into the Yahoo College Literary Review.

But Mary was no match for the vigor that shot sparks from Hilda's blue eyes. She eventually gave the persistent woman her phone number, and apologized to Tonio's regulars, "I think she had too much of the house red. Imagine 'the bomber's seed approaching the world's ripe womb' ending up as plainsong in a village church."

She was surprised when Hilda called and invited her to dinner. "And bring some of your work to read. I'm asking a few people over who want to hear it."

But neither of the odd couples who showed up at the old farmhouse near the ocean paid Mary's poetry the slightest attention. The young minister argued throughout dinner for importing an activist nun to preach on South Africa. His wife, a computer programmer, interrupted him at regular intervals to complain about the church's real need — a PC to make the office work more efficient. The ancient deacon muttered and moaned about dwindling attendance and contributions. Hilda was not put off by their disinterest in Mary. Between the roast lamb and the cherry cobbler, she convinced the minister and the deacon that the nun should speak on nuclear disarmament, accompanied by Mary's "Sign of Shock." "And I'll start a fund-raiser for the computer," she promised the minister's wife.

Mary remembers the group's air of resignation; it spoke of losing many battles to Hilda's will. Soon, Mary was in a state of shock herself. As they carried the dessert dishes back to the kitchen, Hilda invited her to come live in the farmhouse, in a cozy attic room with a tiny fireplace. "I need my collaborator right here with me," she said. "I don't charge much rent, and my two kids, Whit and Julie, need somebody smarter than me to help them with their homework."

Mary had looked into the eyes of this creature who seemed determined to change her life. She remembers how Hilda had boldly stared back, the enlarged pupils of her blue eyes as deep and inviting as a summer lake. She had patted Mary's cheek. "We're both going to enjoy this," she had said, at Mary's unspoken question.

A large bluefish gasps in the sand at Mary's feet. She examines the monster. It is the exact shade of the greasy sky.

Hilda puts her foot on the fish to halt its struggles, and with a small pair of pliers twists the barbed hook from its mouth. Mary has read that fish have such small brains they feel no pain. She hopes this is so, for she fancies she hears a scream as Hilda rips the hook out. The blue lunges at her friend's hand in its final frenzy.

Hilda notes Mary's distress. "Blues are mean and unpredictable, fighters right up to the end. But it'll be dead in five minutes," she says. "Cast out again. You'll get the next one."

I'm nowhere near the fighter that bluefish was, Mary thinks. She turns away from the dying fish and makes another fumbling cast. Because I was lonely in my small pond, because I was hungry for change, because I wanted to take one last chance before routine became decay, Hilda hooked me with barely a struggle. Now I, who had never entered a church in my life, am happily making joyful noises for potato farmers and Toyota salesmen. When the feeble choir of Grace Church meekly sings "Sign of Shock" and "Underwater," a call to preserve *Roe v. Wade*, the congregation rejoices with the same enthusiasm as the crowd at Tonio's. It's still recovering from Hilda's last project, setting some erotic passages from "The Prophet" to Handel's *Water Music*. Mary, though small, dark, and intellectual, is still not as foreign as Kahlil Gibran.

She bares her beautiful teeth at the ocean and once more, ineptly, reels in her line.

Hilda tosses the sharp-toothed fish into the bucket with the others and rejoins her friend at the edge of the sea. Her affection for Mary, for those thin shoulders and frail body leaning out into the horizon, moves her to prayer. Hilda thanks God regularly and sincerely. Hadn't He helped her get rid of a useless husband whose only passions were Italian shoes and European au pairs?

God has got to help one more time. He has delivered to her a companion, collaborator, and lover. With little persuasion, she was able to convince Mary of their compatibility, their mutual needs, their oneness in a miserable world. Mary is her first female lover and, to Hilda's mind, far superior to the males she has bailed out of funks and failures. Hilda understands that her comeliness attracts the opposite sex like a Patriot to a Scud, but she is tired of the nonstop nurturing.

On the nights when the kids are asleep and she clambers up to Mary's bedroom in her flannel nightgown, she slides into the warmth of Mary's arms with a blissful sigh. Mary is a totally new product, in a vastly improved wrapper. She is a quite satisfactory answer to Hilda's physical needs, and their collaboration at church seems to Hilda to be the most inventive idea she has ever had, even better than the corkscrew hook.

And Mary, unlike those panting, doglike men, is a well-bred Siamese, content to be left alone. When she isn't teaching, she spends a lot of time in the attic writing and thinking. This is in happy contrast to Hilda's former husband, for instance, whom she faulted for attending too diligently to the 18-year-old babysitter and Belle Scarpe Shoesalon than to his real estate business. Otherwise, he haunted the refrigerator, complaining that they were out of Corona Extra again — and what did Hilda expect, when she kept neglecting him for her bubba fishing mania? When she caught her husband assaulting Elke the sitter under the dining room table, she went ballistic.

Six months ago, two years after her divorce and a recent breakup with yet another boyfriend, Hilda became intrigued with Tonio's. On the beach, she overheard a conversation about the bookstore's social evenings, featuring, along with literary renditions, a number of semidetached men. She decided to take the next opportunity to look around.

But she forgot to concern herself with the three males who showed up for the poetry reading. Her social life gave way before Mary's face, which touched Hilda's heart and mind far more than her verses. Hilda thought Mary looked as forlorn as the orphans Sally Struthers and Mary Tyler Moore promoted in the magazine ads. A blue vein in the poet's temple beat time as she read. Here was someone who appeared to need immediate, remedial help. Hilda decided to ignite both Mary's poetry and her life. Tonio's matchmaking would have to wait.

"Help her God, please help her," she now enjoins the sky where the sickly sun is sliding away from her vision. "You won't be sorry." Although Hilda has rediscovered that

every commitment carries a price, she is not yet ready for
solitary confinement.

Mary's next cast finally sends the line somewhat beyond the
breakers pounding the shore. She relaxes a bit. "Practice," she
thinks. "The mystique disappears with practice, just like
poetry."

"Good cast, keep it up," says Hilda. "But what about
your feet? Aren't they getting cold and wet?"

A couple of inches of seawater are sloshing around in
her inadequate rain boots, but Mary doesn't answer. Her
pride and budget do not permit either a loan of waders from
Hilda or a purchase, and she resents Hilda's inference of her
dependency.

"I'm perfectly okay, Hilda," Mary retorts, turning her
back on her friend. Hilda has become somewhat of a bore
lately. Those country breakfasts of sausages and pancakes, the
little fireplace always made up and ready to light, Hilda's
boisterous love and affection, at first so freely and happily
given, more and more seem to be demanding all sorts of
reciprocation. Mary finds herself designated the official
homework consultant for Whit and Julie, having to make
herself available every night for advice on Captain Ahab and
square roots. In her past incarnation, evenings had been
sacred, for work; she often wrote her best poems at midnight.

And Hilda, who spends her evenings watching TV or
out playing poker, has recently asked Mary to babysit,
without a word about where she's going. Whit and Julie,

unconcerned, use their mother's absence to play Metallica at maximum volume in spite of Mary's protests. "Lighten up, Mary," they say, "If Mom doesn't care, why should you?" When Mary isn't beseeching the kids to turn down the stereo, she tries to wheedle from them the truth of Hilda's whereabouts. "Who knows? Mom's a space case," is their answer. "Don't sweat it. We don't."

But she is not of the children's laissez-faire temperament, and Hilda's secretiveness is only one of Mary's anxieties. More and more, she feels like the third of Hilda's children, as Hilda directs her schedule, plans their lives, plays the maestro to Mary's first violin. When Hilda comes to her late at night, whispering words of love, Mary is temporarily appeased. Hilda is as intense a lover as she is a politician. She strokes Mary's hair and whispers, "My very own poet laureate; I'm so lucky." Then, she falls asleep while Mary tosses. It's true her recent poetry seems softer, more lyrical, less angular and intense. But she misses the warm rain of applause that once richocheted off Tonio's tin ceiling. She has been too busy with church hymns to give the lecture hall much time. She worries that relationships are too confining, as demanding to the spirit as nine-to-five jobs.

At Hilda's insistence, she began to learn to fish. Hilda was dedicated to instilling in her some practical education, Mary realized, as if while she was proud of Mary's art, she still saw it as a product of a flaky intellectual. A sport would help Mary balance priorities, temper the agony, the depression of creation.

Mary thinks, I've always hated physical work or sports, but if I can only catch a fish today, perhaps it will quiet the fluttering that's recently been disturbing my insides. But working to prove to Hilda that she is more than a complaisant lover, only adept at hymn lyrics and comfort on cold nights, stirs up the flutter again. I wonder if her husband felt this way, too, she thinks, if Hilda's matter-of-fact capability made him defensive, made him feel less than independent, less than a man.

Mary concentrates on letting her lure drop toward the sandy bottom and then reeling it in, steady, no jerking motions, as Hilda has taught her. She has to admit that Hilda has widened the avenues of her previously constricted life — taught her how to draw to a straight flush, for instance, how to make a pesto omelet, to sing out harmoniously in choir. There's a pull on the line, and Mary grips her rod anxiously.

"Something's there," she whispers to Hilda, as if the fish might hear and take itself off.

"Keep reeling slowly, then give a small jerk for a test," says Hilda. Mary's face, white and pinched, reminds her of a child's on Christmas morning.

But when Mary reels again, the line is slack. The fish has slipped the hook.

❊ ———————— ❊

Hilda is in the middle of offering up another prayer when her own rod begins to bend alarmingly, almost pulling out of her hands. "Holy Jesus, this is a big mother," she calls to Mary. Hilda concentrates hard. This time, she will have a good run. She grins at the sea.

The bass, for sure that's what it is, is playing the line cleverly. It will not tire as easily as the bluefish. It will play dead, go limp in the water, give up struggling. When the angler stops reeling, it will heave with all its strength and take off like a streak, hoping to snap the 15-pound test line. Hilda is wise to this trickery, and loosens the drag to give the line more play. The bass moves parallel to the shore. Hilda must follow it or lose it.

Then she remembers Mary and looks over her shoulder. Her friend is sitting at the edge of the dune, pouring sea-water from her boots. She is struggling to disentangle a fouled line. Her eyes are tearful.

"Mary," calls Hilda in sudden inspiration, "want to land this sucker?"

Mary seems about to shake her head, then pulls on her soggy boots and runs over to her friend at the shoreline.

Hilda passes the rod to Mary. "Keep a tight grip on it, with your fingers splayed over the holder, so . . . Let up on the tension, yes that's right, counterclockwise, so the bugger can run with it. But he's smart, smarter than a bluefish, and he'll play dead when you least expect it, and then whammo, off he goes, and snap! Adios, line."

Fire burns into the small of Mary's back, her feet are as cold as a cadaver's, and more water rushes into her boots. Like claws into flesh, her fingers embed themselves in the rod. She repeats the instructions — "Let it run, watch the tension, go with it" — then follows the big fish up the beach as first it bolts and then stops dead in its wily flight.

Is the hook set, she wonders anxiously, as she stumbles and plods along the greasy shore. Is the barb sunk enough into the fish's jaw to hold during this interminable journey that seems longer than any I've ever taken? To keep up her spirits, she recites the names of lures, "Spinners, wobblers, plugs, lead-head jigs. Spinners, wobblers, plugs . . ."

The bass changes tactics and direction. Mary plods back along the shore. She is shivering and her feet are like ice. But she seems to be playing the line more expertly, sticking the rod butt between her legs for better leverage when the bass pauses in its crazy run, getting the feel for when to reel in the line a bit more, and when to give it more play. She senses that slowly she is winning the battle between herself and this monster that is challenging her.

The old grumbler, Charley, appears beside her. He has changed his tune. "Hang in there, sister. Don't let the bastard get the best of you. Show him who's boss."

Show him who's boss. It seems possible that she can do just that. Perhaps, just perhaps, she is at last learning the secrets of physicality, will one day marry physical prowess with intellectual. Mary's formerly bound and constricted heart beats easier. Her breath, instead of bursting in short jerks, is slower, more controlled. She looks around for Hilda's approval. Strange that Hilda is allowing her to play in the fish alone, not capering about, shouting advice, rooting for Mary in this fiendish contest of wits and strength.

"Hilda, I think I'm getting it," Mary calls out to the now-friendly landscape. Over her head, a cluster of clouds, a puffy pewter blanket, closes off what little daylight remains.

No answer, and Mary steps back from the breaking waves, peers over her shoulder into the gloom.

She spots Hilda silhouetted against the darkening sky at the top of a rise. A man is with her, unfamiliar. His rod and Mary's stand beside them in their spikes, swaying like magic wands. His hands and Hilda's are entwined. They might be beginning a dance. Their lips meet like their hands, and the two figures, two parts of a human origami, meld together identical down vests and peaked caps.

Mary sucks in her breath. A metronomic pain, much uglier than the flutter, begins to beat in her chest. The bass, as if intuiting a faltering adversary, summons its strength into a massive heave, darts away from Mary in a last dash for freedom. Mary, taken by surprise, stumbles forward into a breaking wave, loses her balance, and tumbles. The force of the autumn sea churns her upside down, fills her nostrils with sand. She gasps and sucks in the mixture, choking, choking, unable to cough it out or get her breath. She tumbles like a toothpick, her inadequate boots like two concrete blocks pulling her toward a watery, inevitable death.

"Not yet!" she burbles, consciousness ebbing. But she is aware that hands are grabbing at her, like fishermen reining in a net. A female voice cries, "She's still got it, drag 'em up!" Mary and the bass are floating away in the strangling sea, into an unconsciousness pillowed by warmth. Then, someone pounds her back, forcing her to cough and protest. Someone else is trying to pry her icy fingers from the rod.

❀ —————— ❀

An hour later, wrapped in an old wool blanket Hilda keeps in the station wagon for emergencies, Mary is being driven home in style. Hilda, at the wheel, holds her hand tightly, humming "Sweet Victory," a recent collaborative hymn celebrating the defeat of a development near the ice-skating pond. "Rushes and phragmites sing their praises / Call to the geese that will nevermore roam."

In the back of the wagon, with Mary's soaked jeans and underwear, lie four blue fish, already scaled and cleaned, and a 45-pound ("at least," Hilda assures) striped bass, as pristine in death as an Egyptian pharaoh. Resplendent on ice, the striper will lie in state in the fridge tonight. Tomorrow morning, the angler and her catch will be photographed for the local paper.

But Mary can't ignore the thudding pain in her head from which she had been free for six months. The headache, which in the past could only be assuaged by three Fiorinals, has interfered often with the creative process, and sometimes frightened her into imagining a brain tumor, not just the migraine the doctor diagnosed. She stifles a yell.

Hilda, unaware, stops humming, bubbles, "We'll have a party. We'll ask every guy on the beach tonight and still have leftovers with this one. I know a great recipe to stuff it with apples and junk. I'll bet old stripey is the biggest of the season. Mary, you're an A-number-one fine-ass fisherman. Those guys are goin' to haveta pay you some respect from now on."

She squeezes Mary's hand and starts again on "rushes and phragmites." Mary is silent. The last hour — the fear of drowning, of losing the fish — has exhausted her. She savors the slaps on the back she received after she got her breath back, realized she was going to live, the congratulations — "See you tomorrow, Mary, gotta prove it wasn't beginner's luck" — Hilda stripping her from her soaking garments and tucking her in the blanket.

She forces out of her cracked lips, "It was lovely of you to take such good care of me tonight, but who was that man . . . ?"

Hilda interrupts, "I couldn't let you freeze to death while I cleaned those fish, could I?" She bounces in her seat. "Whit and Julie won't believe this. They've been trying for a striper for five years. Now, they'll know you can do anything."

Mary draws the blanket closer. "I saw you on the dunes. Just before I fell. With a man. Kissing him. What does that mean?"

Hilda clears her throat as if she is about to make a speech, then pauses. "It was . . . a guy I haven't seen in a while. From before we met. He's just come back to town. Just an old fishing buddy."

Mary reflects on the lie. Hilda is bad at mendacity; evasiveness is her stock in trade. An old fishing buddy you've been sneaking off for weeks to see, leaving me at home with your metal-head children. Mary says, as if changing the subject back to the bass adventure, "I think I'll quit while I'm ahead."

"What do you mean?"

"I mean that I won't be doing any more fishing."

"But, Mary," from the driver's seat an incredulous voice drifts toward her, "You can't mean that. You've just caught the biggest fish of your life, and you've learned . . ."

Mary smiles to herself. The thudding pain is easing.

"You don't understand, Hilda, I've been neglecting my work for this silly sport."

Sounds of heavy breathing and anxious stirrings.

"But I — I thought you liked it, the beach, the birds, the guys, learning something new. And you learned so well, you di-did outfish them . . ."

Mary feels another victory about to happen. She imagines the crowd at Tonio's cheering, urging her on. A good performance is a skill she has perfected without Hilda's help.

She pats Hilda's hand. "I really don't even like the sport, to tell you the truth. I thought I would, but it's ridiculous goofing off all day with a lot of ne'er-do-wells. And I don't see anything romantic about fishermen, as you apparently do."

She notes Hilda's silence. "Yes, I think I should definitely quit this game on a high note."

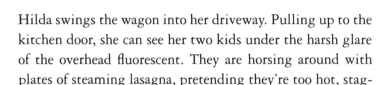

Hilda swings the wagon into her driveway. Pulling up to the kitchen door, she can see her two kids under the harsh glare of the overhead fluorescent. They are horsing around with plates of steaming lasagna, pretending they're too hot, staggering as they bear them to the kitchen table.

Bless Julie and Whit; she'll thank them kindly for remembering to turn on the oven. They're getting more responsible; soon, they'll be adults. Perhaps they've even set the table. How delicious the lasagna will taste, with a glass of red wine, and the salad she made early in the day. She is glad she defrosted the lasagna. The kids hate fish.

In her mind, a vision blooms. A woman, no longer young, is alone in a country kitchen. The house inside is as quiet as the desolate landscape. Hilda gulps back tears. She wrenches the cooler from the back of the wagon, and slams the top down. "Let's see how you feel tomorrow."

Mary ignores Hilda's bid for reconciliation. The ebullience of success, the headiness of revenge has quieted those inner flutterings that she thought were permanent, like high blood pressure or varicose veins. Even the pounding headache is settling down to a dull ache. Now that she is a power to not one but two groups of necessary acolytes, her life seems complete, her personality newly integrated. For the first time, she has shifted from manual to automatic, ceased bucking and jerking down the road of life. It wasn't, after all, too difficult to learn to fish.

Mary, now, is as anxious as Hilda to step inside the welcoming house, but not to bask in adolescent acclaim. She will accept a glass of wine, accept Whit and Julie's congratulations calmly, then tell them she is too tired for lasagna or to help with tonight's homework. To Hilda she will say she must go directly to bed, her head is killing her, she must medicate and then sleep off the day's tension.

Hilda will understand those excuses; they are legitimate after a successful, stressful day. Mary will hurry to her attic room, take two Fiorinals, pull out the bottle of Chianti stored in her cupboard. Soon, she will be free of pain. And then, as an artist first and foremost, it will be her duty, her responsibility to herself to begin a record of the afternoon's events in her notebook. Such intense illumination must not go unremarked. All that has gone before was but raw material, mere preparation for the ripe maturity of her talent.

As the two women open the kitchen door, blinking a little in the warmth and the light, Mary has already outlined the first four lines of her newest, most life-affirming poem. She has decided to entitle it, "Getting the Blues."

See It My Way

❀ ———————————— ❀

I went to visit Gloria at Riverside Hospital today. She had made herself up for me, lipstick and blusher enscribed like hex signs on her pale face.

Yesterday, Dr. Albert eyeballed me solemnly across his desk. The feeble strands of his hair transplant marched across his scalp, like corn rows in need of fertilizer, distracting me from his admonitions. "Your mother is terminal," he said. "A week at most."

Gloria was propped up in bed, waiting for me, pretending to read *National Geographic.* "Take a break," she said to Mrs. deLisle, her Haitian nurse, with whom I sometimes practiced my school French.

"*Fatigue pas ta mère,* she's had a very difficult day," Mrs. deLisle cautioned, heading for the cafeteria.

Gloria was annoyed at the French. "She only speaks English to me," she complained.

"Because she doesn't want you to expend any extra energy," I said.

"It isn't my brain that's sick," she said, and pointed to a picture of Cairo, Egypt, in the magazine.

"See how beautiful the city looks here? It's the crummiest, dirtier than New York if that's possible, choking under a layer of dust as old as the pyramids, beggars clutching at your body as soon as you leave the hotel, panhandling even in the museum. Everybody lies these days, including old friends like the *National Geo.*"

Gloria stopped, the tiny outburst dampening her forehead, the effort to stay alert a last round of her unruly will.

I gave her some ice — she's not eating — while she got her breath back. The radiator clanked under the dirty window. The TV, flickering night and day from its post on the wall, beamed us with its benign eye. No one visits Gloria but me. She is as neglected as her room.

Even Mick has given up making the effort. Sometimes he gets as far as the entrance hall, where a chapel and the florist's dyed carnations vie for last minute atonement. But he always stops. "You go on up, Liz, I can't quite face it."

"Forget the *National Geo.*" I swabbed Gloria's brow with a Kleenex. A smell like a mildewed closet rose from the bed. "Only rubes read it. I'm going to bring you *Playgirl* tomorrow."

Gloria looked at me hard. "Did you know," she said, her lips stretched across teeth as big as tombstones in her shrunken face, "that I haven't had sex in more than a year? And now, I'm too sick to miss it. When George Mason was in the shape I am, maybe worse, he asked his day nurse to give him a blow job. I don't know whether she did or not, but he got well, and when he went home, he left Alma for the nurse. What do you think?"

I said, "Well, just don't attack the guy who waxes the floor."

If she did, it would only be the latest of Gloria's riveting experiences with the world of medical science. Other kids' mothers read them *Winnie the Pooh* and *Babar*. Gloria terrified my brother, Mick, and me with stories of the Grim Reaper. Like what happened to Uncle Ben, carried to Riverside when he was hit by a car on West End Avenue. Two days later, his head bandaged and his broken leg in a cast, he was laughing at one of Gloria's Polish jokes when he stopped, muttered, "Oh, no," fell back on the pillows, and died. Gloria complained her joke wasn't that bad. To tease us, she repeated it while we held our breaths, fearful that our appreciation, like Uncle Ben's, would smite us fatally.

"There was this Polish terrorist who tried to blow up a bus. But he had to stop when he burned his mouth on the tail pipe." Gloria guffawed and we longed to imitate her toughness.

Our mother's strength had been our rabbit's foot, charming us into believing that by treating physical weakness as subversive, we could live forever. Now that Gloria had filed herself away with the other unfortunates, we were bewildered and angry.

Hadn't we learned early that hospitals meant horror, not healing? Even Riverside, a giant with a dazzling reputation for top-notch medicine, featured in too many obituaries. It reminds me of a setting for an old prison movie, where the jailbird shuffles down miles of polished corridor before the cell door clangs behind him. Riverside employs guards with guns, just like Sing Sing.

Gloria never mentions Mick's absence. Maybe she remembers his nightmares after our father's one hospitalization.

Mick was 13 then, when our father, recovering from a wrenched back on the tennis court, shared room 22 at Beekman Downtown with a man named Harold, hit head-on in his little Ford by a stoned teenager in a stolen pickup. Father was not sympathetic. He said that anyone who snored as loud as Harold couldn't be in that much pain. Mick hung his pubescent lankiness over Harold's footboard and talked to him about soccer teams. Harold gave Mick a tattered photo of Pelé as a teenager.

One day they amputated Harold's right leg. Then, Mick and Harold discussed one-legged athletes. Mick, his face alight with the possibilities of dangerous knowledge, asked Harold to show him his stump. Gloria dragged Mick out from behind the shielding curtain just in time.

The day we went to bring our father home, we found Harold's bed empty. Father said that while he was trying on his new orthopedic corset in the bathroom, Harold had hoisted himself out of bed and disappeared down the hall. He opened a window and jumped six stories, leaving his crutches neatly propped against the frame. Our father said he and Harold really hadn't talked much, so he didn't know what was troubling the guy. Mick patted the taut sheets of Harold's newly made bed as if searching for something he'd lost.

As I rolled our father down the hall to freedom, he called for Mick to hurry right along. But Mick was clutching the door of room 22, crying silently. Gloria hovered, passing him Kleenex.

"How about a little massage?" I said to Gloria, who was shifting restlessly beneath her sheets. "No, just lie on the bed with me," she said. "Stop wandering around." Had I been doing that? True, I was staring across the river at the darkening factories of Hoboken, and I had a squashed chocolate in my hand. I put it back in its box, put my glasses next to a bottle of Advil and climbed into bed with Gloria. Her body was hot and dry, like her breath.

"Mick wouldn't like the way I look now, would he?" She stared at me in her tough way, daring me to lie.

I did. "Of course he would, he loves you," I said.

She sighed and breathed on me. "Have you heard anything from your father?"

"He calls every day," I said. "He doesn't want to come unless you want to see him. He thinks it will disturb you."

She sniffed. "How could he disturb me now? He disturbed me a lot last year, but not now. Now, I'd like to feed on his sanity." She hoisted her body up. "Give me a hand. I gotta go to the john."

Like a couple of drunks, she staggering, me supporting her boniness, we moved. I couldn't bear to look at her, the skimpy hospital gown exposing her inflamed buttocks, scabby with bedsores in spite of Mrs. deLisle's ministrations.

"Look at these sticks," she panted, as we struggled the 15 feet to the toilet. "Your father used to say I had the best legs on the East Side."

I had never heard our father compliment Gloria on her legs or anything else, but we made it to the john, where I helped her sit down, then backed out. Did Mrs. deLisle do the same thing, I wondered, or did she stay with her through the grunts and groans in case she fell or fainted?

"Shut the door," she commanded, "all the way."

I sat down on her bed and bit on a ragged cuticle. When had Gloria stopped being obsessive about all of us — our father, Mick, me — and begun to concentrate on herself? She had always preached fairness, but was it fair for her to fight the end so desperately?

Inside the toilet there was a deafening silence. Should I check? Mrs. deLisle had been gone a long time. What if . . . Well, in that case, there'd have to be an obituary, no? I wrote it in my mind, against a background of doubt. "Gloria Rooney, 53, graduate of Wellesley, class of '61, mother of two children, divorced. Artist whose works on cotton and silk are in the collections of the St. Louis Design Center, the Tucson Academy of Art, as well as in private collections. In lieu of flowers, donations may be sent to the National Wildlife Fund." Or something to that effect.

The toilet flushed. "Okay," Gloria said, and I opened the door. Getting her back to the bed was slower than before. It reminded me of being dragged whining and scuffling to school. I hated school. In snow or rain, Gloria would hector me. "Hurry up, for God's sake. Are you a lump of sugar? You won't melt." She was too cheap to hail a taxi, and she made me feel that only a weakling would consider one.

I smoothed her sheets and Gloria closed her eyes. I looked at my watch again. Mrs. deLisle had been gone 30 minutes. What in hell was her problem? Did we pay her these fantastic wages to shoot the breeze while the rest of us suffered? "Mme. Rooney is circling the drain," she would be telling a friend in the cafeteria, her importance enriched by a Danish and strong, black coffee. I bit my cuticle some more.

Mori was sure to be home by now, aggravated because the fridge was empty and I wasn't there, that he'd have to take Finnegan, our Lab, for his evening walk. Mori never visited Riverside, either; he said he made Gloria uncomfortable. She doesn't like me, he said. She thinks I'm too ethnic, just a whiff of Japanese exotica taking up time in your life. She wants a proper son-in-law, a nice Irish lawyer who will give you babies.

That's a pile of it, Mori, I answered back, and you know it. Gloria's too sick to think about anything, especially you. And she loves anyone I love, who makes me happy.

Except I don't these days, he said, and put an end to that conversation.

"Do you want some ice? How about a back rub?" I hovered over Gloria.

"No, just tell me things," she said, not opening her eyes.

Let's see, let me tell you that your illness is exhausting not only the insurance money but your nearest and dearest, that I can hardly drag myself here each day, that my guilts and anxieties are giving me problems at work, that Mrs. deLisle is getting antsy and making noises about leaving. That I'm tired of lying for Mick and our father, and oh Gloria, please, I'm scared.

"Let's see." I bent toward Gloria. She had always appreciated raw, earthy tales. And she had certainly related enough of them to me. "Mori told me this funny story about Sam Leon, you know, his friend, the film producer? It seems that Sam's 11-year-old daughter, Sandy, went to spend the weekend with a school buddy. But Saturday morning early, she called Sam to come get her. Very unusual, as generally she has to be dragged home on Sunday night. Right away, she told him that on her arrival, her friend whisked her off to her father's study. She opened a file cabinet, fished under some account books, and drew out a pile of dirty magazines. She said to Sandy, 'Look, they're not your *Penthouse* or *Playboy*, either. They're your *Party Fucking*.' "

I peeked a look at Gloria. Her normal horselaugh had sunk into deep, black water. Could I bring it to the surface once more? Mori was aghast at the absence of convention between Gloria and me. I think he found it faintly disgusting, soiling his notions of generational piety. I hurried on.

"And that's not the worst. While the kids were engrossed in the magazines, the folks came back from wherever. So, the girls stuffed the mags into a pillowcase, just in time. They finally managed some fake yawns and said they'd go to bed. But Sandy grabbed the pillowcase upside down and the porn fell out in front of Mom and Dad. Sandy's friend screamed, 'She made me do it.' Then, Dad gave the two girls a stiff lecture about respect for privacy. Sandy said to Sam, 'How's that for total crapola?' "

Gloria's body jumped.

"Sam Leon's daughter sounds okay. And how is Mori, anyway?"

"He's good, no change on his script. I think he's working out at the health club tonight."

Mori's three film scripts had yet to find a producer. His professional future, like our relationship, was delicate. His needs were as foreign to Gloria as his heritage, but her interest had an old-fashioned sense of propriety, phony but reassuring.

"Mori is so different from Jack," Gloria said and opened her eyes. Suddenly, they were bright and luminous.

"I guess that's good?" I said.

"Don't mock your father. He did a lotta good things for you."

"He sure taught me to hate cornflakes."

Gloria wasn't listening. "He understood the responsibilities (six syllables were getting too tough, she slurred the word) of fatherhood. More than today's men."

(Okay, Mick, Mori, take your licks. Never going to see either of you pushing the baby carriage, asking friendly neighbors what to do about thumb sucking . . .)

Gloria breathed in bursts. "He wanted you to succeed."

I pictured her, back when we were growing up, her legendary energy. "You wanted us to be happy, I remember."

Gloria was silent. I thought we had exhausted the subject. But then she said, "Crazy. Why aren't you? I was . . ."

"Oh, nobody I know is happy. But my unhappiness isn't heavy-duty. I want you to get well, that would make me really happy."

She sounded vague. "Would it, I wonder?"

Time seemed to have taken a holiday. DeLisle had been gone 40 minutes.

Gloria's eyes were open. She said, "She'll be back soon. Tell me, Mori's not leaving you, is he?"

I hadn't noticed a crystal ball next to the bedpan.

"Of course not, we're fine."

"He's not good enough for you. Not bright enough, not ambitious enough. Fiddling around with those special effects . . ."

Why couldn't I think of something to change the subject?

"As good as most of the stuff you see on TV nowadays."

"Not so. Your father has talent, imagination." She sighed. "I wish he were here right now. Since he left, I've really had no one to talk to."

Maybe that's the way it is with sick people, they receive

a last burst of energy from the Holy Ghost, so as to rise up from their beds of pain to kick you in the guts. In her final agony, Gloria craved an audience with our father, Jack Rooney, the Autocrat of the Breakfast Table.

"Okay, sports fans, this morning I'm going to tell you about New York City's fiscal crisis." Or the complete roster of the Miami Dolphins, plus characteristics of the constellations and names of Marx Brothers costars.

"God, Dad, can't we just eat our cereal in peace?"

"Nonsense, you can walk and chew gum, can't you? Let me tell you about Eddie Koch's deal with the West Village Independent Democrats."

Mick and I sat in mute fury, forbidden to leave the table until after the quiz, which followed the lecture. Gloria, a loyal soldier, listened carefully and wrinkled her brow in concentration, but our father never called on her. Finally, she would get Mick excused on some pretext or other. When I protested, she said, "You're tougher than your father. Hang in. Don't let him bully you."

Now, Gloria was licking her dry lips. "I want some ice. And . . . I want to see Jack. I want to tell him something before I die. Will you get him here?"

I cocked my ear for sounds outside. Wait until deLisle comes back, I'll give her unshirted hell. I fed Gloria the calming cubes and stared at the TV. The six o'clock news was flickering. Two blow-dried mannequins were miming the detritus of the day, and I couldn't get the joke.

"Liz, Liz, listen . . . Promise me." Gloria fumbled around on the bed for my hand, grabbed it in her chicken's claw. Behind her eyes a fire burned. Who's going to quench that flame? Not Jack Rooney, with his new wife and baby, his immortality renewed. He won't come within a block of this chamber of horrors.

"I promise, I promise, take it easy, Gloria. Look, try to rest a little and I'll make a phone call to see if I can raise him."

She lay back and I whisked out the door and looked hopefully down a corridor as long as a football field. The glistening vinyl seemed to have been waxed since I walked on it less than an hour ago. Somewhere in the distance I could hear giggles, faint music. Somewhere down there healthy people were laughing and listening to the Top Ten. Down there was a tie-line to crowds and crime and life. I hurried.

A young doctor, his stethoscope a dangling virility symbol, scampered away from the nurses' station and down the hall. Feeling up the nurses. I was jealous.

I skidded to a halt near the station. It was empty except for a little dark nurse poring over her charts. Linda Ronstadt was singing "What's New" on a small portable, but the reception wasn't clear. I eyed the telephone booth, but I didn't go near it.

I started to shuffle back toward 1216. Halfway there, a sound, like the toll of a long-silent clock, reached me. It was one of Gloria's tales, being retold.

"Oh-h, oh-h, God, he-lp me, he-lp me." A scream trickled down the hall.

Gloria was struggling to clear herself of the bedsheets as I flung open the door. She was retching. "Go find Mrs. deLisle, hurry!"

"In a minute, what's the matter, what's wrong? Can I do something?"

Gloria had her feet over the edge of the bed. "Go find her or I will," she cried, then fell back across the bed.

This time I flew down the hall, a long, thin scream fluttering like a kite's tail on my heels. A couple of open doors along the hall closed, fending off demons.

"Quick," I yelled, startling the Filipino nurse, who had put away her charts and was bathing in *Cosmo*'s prescriptions for a better body and astounding love life. I ran around the counter and grabbed her. The name tag said H. Barbaza, R.N. "It's my mother, Mrs. Rooney, she's in trouble."

H. Barbaza, R.N., closed the magazine after turning down the page, and looked at her watch. Another scream flew down the hall. I cowered against the station counter and watched the lights flicker. I was going to faint right there on the Johnson's Glo-Coat.

"Black bitch," the nurse pronounced, opening the door of the refrigerator in her little arena. Then she squeaked purposefully down the hall, me trailing her like a raw recruit behind the point man. "Stay out a minute," she flung over her shoulder, and pushed open 1216.

I counted to 60 slowly, then plunged in. The floor nurse had Gloria turned on her side, her raw buttock feeding on a needle the size of a ballpoint. The yelps of pain were turning into groans; the elixir was working. The nurse was taking Gloria's pulse. Gloria's face was unrecognizable, a melting mask of sweat and agony. Her eyes were open, but she was gazing at something horrible.

"Will she be all right?"

The nurse grunted, removed the hypo, rolled Gloria on her back. She made an entry on the chart at the foot of the bed.

"I'd better have deLisle paged," was all she said.

The door swung open to the Magic Kingdom. Mrs. deLisle stood there, taking in the situation, me cowering, the huffy nurse, Gloria a bundle of trash ready for the bin. She looked untroubled, ready to deal with crises. Gloria stirred at the sound.

"Jack," she said, fixing her milky gaze on her savior, extending her hand like a hostess in a receiving line. "It's so nice of you to come stay with me while I die."

Mrs. deLisle put down her purse and the *Post*, and sat on the bed. She folded Gloria's hands into her own strong black ones. "I'm here, *ma petite*," she said. "I'm sorry it took me so long."

"Doesn't matter," muttered Gloria. "I knew you wouldn't leave me."

H. Barbaza, R.N., had disappeared without a word. Mrs. deLisle began to stroke Gloria's forehead. Gloria twisted her mouth and closed her eyes. They were a symbiotic duo, the complete cast of a two-character play.

Mrs. deLisle finally noticed me. She smiled. "*Retourne demain*," she said. "Your maman will be better, I know. *Et, ferme la lumière quand tu pars.* Okay?"

Ça va.

I struggled down the corridor against towering tufts of corn silk. At the nurses' station, the radio was sounding off unctuously, "Today, Margaret Thatcher, the former Iron Lady of Great Britain, affirmed her support . . ." I leaned against the counter; my legs had sprung a leak. H. Barbaza looked up expectantly. For the first time, I noticed a sign on her desk. It read, "Save time. See it my way."

Honor Is the Subject

❀ ——————————————————— ❀

*D*ear Dr. Goldie Makeover, about once a week I think seriously of suicide. Thirty-five years old and still holding over the runway of life. I could like split and head west, but where? California's got more nuts than Brazil.

"Vot cleffer inzights vee pull out uff our hats."

Call me Sis the Missed; I'm attracting the worst kind of karma possible. See, Dr. MakeMeOver, sometimes it's a really sad thing, I find myself partying in apartments bigger than Grand Central, invited by mistake to rooms deodorized with Brie wax and money.

"Take a vrisk!"

I'm being jerked around by everybody, by Miss Winpenny, who doesn't think I can teach English to her student morons, when I was top D-O-G in E. Lit and Dr. Baron used to tell me so in those afternoon sessions in his office with the door locked. He was a toad, not a Mr. Darcy at all, but I graduated cum laude. That and my mom's long friendship with Winpenny got me the job at Gordon School.

I was psyched; imagine getting paid to live with Camus and Roskolnikov. It only took me six months to discover I was being paid to baby-sit bimbos — pretty, rich girls whose interest in Mr. Darcy is as remote as Geraldo's in Kafka. Angst!

"Iss not ze decline off vestern cifilisation."

And the brain-dead parents who invite me to their posh parties just to jerk me around over dessert. ("Now, Ms. Adams, we're not mega-happy with Dolores's grades. Especially when we've been encouraged to donate big bucks to the new gym. Hey, it's only high school.")

"Iss more simply ze matter of ferbal dexterity."

But I'm bent out of shape the most when I'm making love to Sid. There we are, hot as Miami in August, with Sid moaning toward his climax. And I'm like crying, I mean really dropping a cloud, gulping and gagging. Over the radio comes the news that gold is selling for $350 an ounce. Sid climbs out of his nosedive and calls his broker.

"Perhaps ve are getting into ze royal road of ze unconscious."

Dear Dr. Makelove, why do our good intentions fade like sepia photographs? Why am I groping through cobwebs? Why is everyone coshed except me and thee, and sometimes I suspect thee?

"Iff a patient has guts, she can stand up to ze pressures uff terapy."

Dear Dr. Makesense, when I told Sid I believed in serial monogamy, he rolled off me and said that's great, real great, Sis, you sure know how to hurt a fellow. Of course, Sid is paranoid because he's only a gorgeous plumber. My last boyfriend was a real intellectual — a disc jockey for WRAT. All day he spun retro platters. "Ave Maria," "Beach

Blanket Bingo," "The Road to Mandalay," anything by Frankie Avalon. Just a little removed from earth, he was. Sid is sweeter, especially if you get off on Lysol.

But if I killed myself, Sid would find another woman quicker than he could locate his hair dryer. Believe me, he did. One night, at a Park Avenue pad with everyone doing coke under an approving Julian Schnabel, Sid took his pants off, kept his mouth shut, and got carted off to Cartagena by a deb into laughing gas. Am I supposed to wait for him to sail back on the Kon Tiki?

"Perhaps you haff set your expectations vay too high."

Dear Dr. Makeamess, like last week, I was bopping up Fifth, the Judds crooning "Why Not Me" into my Walkman, when I saw this guy, he was a boy really, ponytailed and bearded, sketching with a crayon in front of St. Thomas church. The thing is, he was armless, he was holding the crayon between his big toe and the next one. Just watching him switch from red to yellow was awesome. Of course, the drawings were barely legible. I threw five dollars into his Kron candy box, and ran to Rumpelmayer's.

"Nonferbal interpretations are emotionally effasif. Vare-as vords establish a record."

Dear Dr. Makebread, Sid has gone to the Galápagos with the debutante. He sent me a postcard of many large turtles crawling toward the sea. They had laid their eggs and were heading painfully back to their natural habitat. Where is my natural habitat, dear friend? It isn't at Gordon. Miss Winpenny, that fat abuser of children, calls me into her head-mistress's office the other day to chat about my "attitude." What attitude can one have when lecturing material girls about the Brontë sisters? I tell her it's her students' attitude that's at fault. "I teach them but they don't learn," I say.

Later, I pop into Conchy Al's, my favorite pub, for an Absolut on ice. Who should practically knock me down on her way out but Winpenny, looking piggier than ever with her face rosy from margaritas.

"Sis," she says, giving me an intense stare, "have you seen Sally Fried?"

"Well, you won't find her in Conchy Al's," I say nervily. "She's a Christian Scientist, remember?"

Winpenny glares at me through her steaming glasses and smoothes her few wisps of hair. She and Sally Fried, the gym teacher, are definitely making it together. But Winpenny pretends sex is something she sits on.

"You were lecturing me about my attitude," I say, "so I'm paying a trip to my therapist. That sign in the window, it says 'attitude adjustment hour.' "

Winpenny stalks off, muttering, "Sis, your mind is a distant planet."

"For effery vorce dere iss a counter vorce."

Dear Dr. Makemerry, it's been so long since I've heard from Sid, but last night he calls to me in my sleep. I get right up; it's 3 A.M. and I dial his apartment in Rego Park. His answerphone comes on and says, "Hi, you just missed me. I'll call you back as soon as I get in." I shriek across the wires, "Listen to me, there are 30,000 reported suicides in the U.S. every year. Did you know that? *Magna civitas, magna solitudo,* you complete chicken shit." I throw on my sweats and go for a jog along the Drive. I feel so bad, I like prod awake every homeless nodding out on a river-view bench.

"Vat do ve talk about today, my dear, anymore fagina problems?"

Dear Dr. Makealot, I know you're supposed to be my energy source, but what about those T-shirts you wear to therapy? Do you counsel rock stars and titans of industry in T-shirts that say "you toucha my titties i breaka you face?" And it's not exactly encouraging to see plastered across your chest, "New York — only for the strong."

"Haff you alvays hated your parenz?"

Dear Dr. Makepeace, the other day, in the midst of a lesson on Emily Brontë's communist orientation in *Wuthering Heights,* the door to the classroom flew open, and one of my old students, Denise Wheatley, burst in like a quarterback. She was up from Savannah, and wanted to buy me dinner. We had a heartfelt evening, with two nice bottles of Valpolicella, and she confessed she had decided to go New Age and leave her husband and two children. Of course, she ended up in my apartment and in my bed. It was a nice change from Sid; Denise is as plump and comfy as a goose-down pillow. And as a low-risk sex partner, she's extremely erotic. But when I rush home from school the next afternoon, she's taken a walk. I call her at her parents' house, and her mother is totally chilled out. Does New Age discuss sex with a parent? Or maybe I'm not hip to modern cultural mores?

"Insh'allah."

Dear Dr. Makedo, I'm unable to lunch today. There, on my desk at school, for all those wimps to drool over, was another postcard from Sid. The Great Barrier Reef. Australia. The card said, "What a country. Deep down, it's shallow. But you should see the fish, beautiful yellow angels, the color of your eyes." Lydia Lawrence, body by Madonna, income by E. F. Hutton, gives me her most excellent sneer and says, "Gee, Miss Adams, did you poke your finger into the electric outlet?"

"A shtorm vithin da brain."

Dear Dr. Makehay, I find a key that Sid hid in a flour can

just in case, and I boogie over to Rego Park. Nothing to break your back over, and I locate Sid's apartment, a groovy little two-family covered with asbestos shingles. Cute!

I use the key and sneak upstairs, Virgo tidy, no dirty dishes in the sink and all the tapes stacked neatly next to the stereo. I put on some Patsy Cline, and while she's crying cause her daddy said good-bye, I do a private eye number. Sid, the scum, he never left on the spur of the moment.

On his kitchen table is a bag with his plumber's tools. It's a sail bag, crisp and white. Plumbers should use black kits like the one the Gordon janitor carts around when he has to clean the Tampax out of the toilets. I lay the tools out one by one; they're a total design statement. Male and female fittings, L-joints, a faucet that says "Froid," a snake, and a short-handled plumber's friend. I gather up the tools and the Patsy Cline tape and head for the G train. That night I lay the tools all over my bed and get off on the "Lovesick Blues" and the plumber's friend.

"Zee obsessiff-compulsiff syndrome increases with zee depressiff state."

Dear Dr. Makeout, lots of quality time these days in Conchy Al's. It's like home, you know, a big sign over the bar reads, "Conchy Al slept here, there and all over." I order Bahamian barbecued ribs with my Absolut shots, and I always wave hello to the stuffed possum keeping watch from the thatched roof. Winpenny is sometimes hiding behind the Shefflera, but she usually leaves when I come in. Once, she forgets something. He's wearing a black and white Hawaiian shirt with pineapples, over fatigues and paratrooper boots. He says to me, "Hello, sweet thing." And I say, "Just in off the range?"

His eyes are like supernovas about to explode and he's

pointing a cigar at my tits. So I say to him, "Wanna go home?" And he says, "Fuckin' A." It's his major conversational contribution except now and then to mumble about Hitler being alive.

Personally, I'm apolitical, Dr. Gold Dust, but give me a break, this G.I. Joe is so blown away, he must have stumbled into a trench of nuclear waste.

"Organic brain damage to ze ffrontal lobe."

Makes you believe in parthenogenesis, you know, reproduction without copulation? I escape from the dogface with most of me intact, put a padlock on my door, and move in with mom and dad.

"Body veakness iss infectious."

Dear Dr. Makemewell, I'm calling in sick a lot. Winpenny rings up every day and whines into the machine. "Sis, Miss Adams, are you there? We really need to talk. The seniors are behind in *Pride and Prejudice,* and the juniors are seriously lost in present participles."

I stay in bed. Let the weenies shift for themselves, then they'll see how necessary I am. Fuckin' A.

"Our terapeutic alliance iss missink."

Dear Dr. Makebelieve, another postcard from Sid, dateline Okeechobee, Florida: "Alligator bits almost as sweet as your kisses. Armando teaching me to plane."

He's closer, getting nearer, my God, to me. My acne will disappear and I will live in the arms of Sid forever. But who is Armando?

"Da vitness iss abuff suspicion."

Dear Dr. Makefast, Winpenny has me on probation, but I think I will buy a dog, woof, woof, pant, pant, or maybe a gun — let's go hunting — and my mom is practicing understanding. I plait a dark red love knot into my long black hair, while she strokes my forehead and babbles. "You modern women have so many difficult choices," she says. "You need a nice old-fashioned man like your father."

"Romantic love," she says, "is what it's all about." I'm like trying to picture my father as a symbol of courtliness. I remember how we used to eavesdrop outside their bedroom door. Inside, we could hear a squeaky voice pleading, "Kiss my tip."

"Some neurotics jannel emotional turmoil into qvite productiff outlets."

We, the Youthful

On a cold January day in 1986, the congregation of the First Methodist Church of Bereston, Maryland, stilled its whispers and craned its neck at the collection of relatives Fanny James had called forth for her last rites. The family filed up the aisle toward the pulpit, where the substitute minister gazed down at the unfamiliar scene and Fanny greeted her mourners in her best navy-blue silk. Jim and his sister, Topsy, Fanny's stepchildren, well past middle age themselves, approached the coffin. As the furnace below the sanctuary roared into the stillness, they both started. A stench of fuel oil collided with the scent of carnations. The triple-strength eyeglasses on Fanny's nose glittered in protest.

Jim imagined that Fanny's glare was a reaction to the funeral expenses, which she would have deplored as excessive, or to Topsy, threatening mayhem. She was drinking too much. Jim thought he understood his sister's behavior. Her husband, whom Jim hadn't seen more than five times in his sister's 30 years of marriage, and whom he couldn't really picture clearly, had died only a month earlier.

Topsy peered down at Fanny as if inspecting for errors. The congregation rustled. Jim grabbed Topsy's arm. She turned to him and said loud enough to be heard in the back pew, "You don't suppose she'll get up, do you?"

Topsy's relations with her stepmother had never been the closest. Jim's earliest memories were of accusations hurled at top volume amid pitiful protests. "She looks just lovely," he said, strong-arming Topsy into a pew reserved for the family. Everyone settled down, and the rest of the relatives filed past the coffin in silence. Jim watched his cousin Helen bend down and kiss Fanny's chilly brow.

Perfect, he thought, a really great show. The old lady had occupied only scraps of her younger relatives' thoughts for years, but now each was outdoing the other in dramatic goodbyes. Jim had made the trip to the small Tidewater city all the way from Corpus Christi, Texas, where his fourth wife sulked in sullen boredom at being denied a diversion. Jim looked over his sister and his cousins, a covey of arthritis and flab, more excited about Fanny's death and its possible rewards than they had ever been about the woman in her life.

When the funeral director's men came up the aisle and cranked shut the lid of the coffin, Topsy alone seemed relieved that Fanny and her accusing spectacles were hidden from sight. Jim thought that one of the straightest of Topsy's traits was her scorn for the fraudulent.

Yet, he was puzzled. By some fluke, Fanny had chosen as executor of her will Topsy, the stepdaughter she had misused until, confused and disoriented, Topsy had fled her brother, her father, her stepmother, all family ties. Fanny had also, unbelievably, willed her stepdaughter her house, the scene of Topsy's hellish encounters with the sadism of sanctimony.

Fanny had to have been aware of Topsy's distaste for anything reminding her of those early days of suffering. Always, when Topsy arrived in Bereston, she appeared distracted, never staying more than a day or two. Yet, in spite of a good memory for old injuries, Fanny entrusted to the most wounded of her sparring partners the final dispensation of her life.

Now, Topsy was swaying in the pew, tossing her bleached, corkscrewed curls to that inner beat that she always used to defend herself against hostile fire. Her Chloroxed hair and too-tight rayon dress made her resemble a geriatric tart. She had always been an experienced sailor, though, rolling to port and starboard with the rough seas, but never quite hitting the deck. Poor Topsy, Jim thought, 52 years old and still struggling.

The minister had begun his eulogy. "Let us worship God and remember before Him His servant, Fanny James. In the name of the Father and of the Son and of the Holy Spirit. Amen. Let us listen to Scripture from Acts . . . I mean . . . John."

Jim sat up straight. He was determined not to write mortality into *his* life story. He touched his hair, still as black and glistening as a tango dancer's, although he was three years older than his sister. Covertly, he flexed a bicep. It bulged with stringy muscles, unchanged over 35 years. His body was still good enough for certain ladies to exclaim over.

That thought cheered him. He remembered last night and turned in his pew to give Cousin Sallie, behind him, a wink. She frowned in return and cast her eyes down. Sallie, now, Jim liked the way she looked, respectable and cool in a plain black suit, befitting her status as headmistress of a small girls' school outside Chicago. But she really looks best with nothing on, Jim thought, and coughed as eros diverted him from the funeral service.

His feelings were a bit hurt by Sallie's frown. Miss High and Mighty, still full of ideas about what could and couldn't be done. He felt sorry for the little girls she watched over. She'd never turn a blind eye to escapades with riding instructors or local boys. Perhaps she had forgotten her youthful tumult, or was still atoning for it. Still, he couldn't complain about last night. Sallie might be a prune, but her thighs were soft as a peach.

The organ wheezed out the opening bars of "How Great Thou Art," thought to be Fanny's favorite hymn. Cousin Charlie, the one who sang in a barbershop quartet, pealed out in his clear baritone, "Then sings my soul, my Savior God to thee, How great thou art, How great thou art!"

Jim took his mind off Sallie for a moment and joined in. Charlie's pure tones were no match for his own thunderous monotone, perfected after years of Fanny's Sunday-morning nudgings. Jim slid into gear. "O, Lord my God, when I in awesome WONN . . . DER / Consider all the worlds thy hands have made / I see the stars, I hear the rolling THUNNN . . . DER." The stained glass windows shook; the congregation stilled.

Charlie's chubby mouth pouted, and he stopped singing. He glared at Jim, who grinned back. He was not thinking about Charlie, but about love. Funny how we fall away from it, he thought; when Fanny and her house were younger, I couldn't wait to be part of my new family. He had been a kid full of dreams when he met his new stepmother. It had been a thrill to be young and strong, putting his new Charles

Atlas muscles to work repairing the garage roof. And to show off to Sallie, or Sallie Grace Benton as she was known then, Fanny's sister's child, a 16-year-old witch with a musky scent that excited every boy who strayed within a mile of her. But she had been certifiable. His stepmother would have taken the stick to him if he had been the wild March Hare Sallie Grace had been.

Unaccountably, she had been her aunt's favorite. Fanny's affection for her niece had been as ardent as her religious supplications.

It had taken Jim years to get Sallie's attention. He had felt inferior to her in every way and she paid him no mind, until he suddenly became intensely romantic in his sailor's whites, 18 years old and eager to waste the gooks at Inchon. Other women were giving him new pride and self-esteem. But his stepmother disapproved of his dropping out of school to join the Navy.

"Don't let him touch you," Jim had overheard Fanny lecturing Sallie Grace. "He'll never amount to a hill of beans." Jim had misunderstood his stepmother's motives at the time, thought she wanted to protect Sallie from a giddy serviceman's overtures. But he came to understand Fanny better, finally understood her true inner urges. He and Fanny had been the real innocents, neither one understanding the futility of their cherished dreams.

The organ subsided with a groan and the congregation settled back in the pews.

Jim shifted in his seat. Erotomania was chasing away any traces of sorrow. Was there something satanic about sexual arousal in the midst of death? The funeral rites moved him not at all, but remembering Sallie's body, last night exuding that same organic combination of spring grass and dank compost he remembered from his youthful couplings, her scent as completely and always a symbol of life as carnations were of death — recalling the slightly raised cherry birthmark on her knee which, when touched, had always aroused her and, subsequently, himself — almost caused Jim to cry out in the sudden stillness of the church.

He put his hymn book over his bulging lap, and sneaked a glance at Cousin Helen, on the other side of him. Could the corpse kisser detect anything unusual? But Helen was directing her attention altar-ward, between sniffs and snorts into her soaked handkerchief. She's really getting into this, Jim thought; a funeral's more exciting to some folks than their real lives. A good funeral is like a good movie: it gives some people the opportunity to unburden themselves, to moan and cry, not in sorrow for the deceased, but for their own miserable existence that is suddenly being revealed as too nasty and short by half.

Not him, though. He had always preferred the hands-on method of living. Last night at the motel where the family was staying, he had stood outside Sallie's window. Combing her hair in a shortie nightgown, which concealed possibly flabby thighs but left her still-perfect legs in view, she gasped as he let himself in.

"You gotta learn to lock your door," he said. "May be rapists about."

"Jim, for God's sake, are you crazy? There are relatives coming out of the woodwork here," Sallie protested.

"Screw 'em," said Jim. He was lonely and lustful. And she was still the one woman whose body, almost every night of his life, was palpable in his arms. "Have you gotten better since the last time?"

Afterward, he laid his bony cheek next to hers and

wondered how many tumbleweeds like him Sallie had taken on over the years. But he said, "Baby, you're more fun than the ponies." His stringy muscles lay softly now across her chest. Was she impressed or repelled by the fierce eagle tattoo on his left bicep, the one that danced when he was excited?

She only rolled out from under him and said, "I have postcoital depression. Would you please leave?"

"I will if you'll marry me," he said, snuggling into her neck. "I can't wait another 35 years."

She had leapt from the bed. "You don't have to marry every woman you sleep with these days. And what about Belle, isn't that the name of wife number four or is it five?"

His chest swelled at the hint of jealousy. "Oh, yeah, Belle, the belle of Corpus Christi. Well, I gotta have somebody push my wheelchair, right?"

When Sallie slammed the door of the bathroom, Jim slowly put on his clothes. "Don't forget that lilac bikini," she had called through the door. He was proud he could still wear a G-string. But this morning before the funeral, she had ignored him completely.

The Baptist preacher, the last-minute sub for Fanny's own pneumonia-stricken Methodist leader, was reinforcing his reputation for absentmindedness. He was young, barely out of the seminary. He had only known Fanny by sight. If she could rise out of that box, she would give him what-for, Jim thought; Fanny believed that the word of God should be delivered with authority, the better to render sinners awestruck and feeble. The minister gamely swung into, "And the glory of her life that is now hidden from us will shine above . . . will shine across . . . will shine *on* the face of God."

What did that space case know about glory, especially

Fanny's? Life was all about luck, anyway, not glory. Jim felt he had had his share of aces for a guy with no education. After Korea, he'd gone into the merchant marine and retired as a full commander. On his best days, he could park a three-block-long oil tanker as neatly as he parked his VW.

And luck with women? Jim thought about Sallie's profile, still good except for a melting chin. A lotta luck and good times with four wives, and assorted others along the way. But not with Fanny. Lady Luck had withheld the cards there. Fanny had been as stingy to him with the glory of her life as with her worldly goods. He went over his thousand-dollar bequest again, his only share of the estate other than a glass-framed carving of a three-master, sails set, that had been his grandfather's. The thousand bucks would just cover his round-trip fare from Corpus Christi. The rest of the family, what Fanny called her blood kin, would come in for lots of good, hard cash.

And Topsy had inherited Fanny's house, that white clapboard and brick edifice that to Jim represented the stability that carried him throughout the world and throughout his life. The place where Fanny, whom he had loved, had once reached out to him. I guess she regretted it, he thought, just as she regretted being hateful to Topsy. At the end, she decided to adjust the scales.

Jim told himself not to agonize. He was not coming away empty-handed. He had had a chance to pay his respects to the mementos of his youth.

The preacher called out the names of the relatives in a commemoration of the dead. But Jim was lost in those times, now as ancient as most of the congregation, when he often sneaked into Sallie Grace's bedroom. On her dresser, a photograph of her Aunt Fanny, a 1914 adolescent framed in ivory, had watched them, an exotic stranger overseeing their fumblings. In long blond curls and a ruffled dress that antique stores now charged a fortune for, she smiled wistfully at a goofy-looking soldier in puttees and AEF hat.

It was the first time Jim had glimpsed a younger Fanny, a woman as corporeal as Sallie. When he first met his stepmother, she was already 40, her gratitude at finally marrying his father tempered by a zealot's devotion to the future righteousness of her charges. Had guilt given birth to that whip of harsh discipline under which he and Topsy had writhed? It hadn't been maternal love that imposed it. Gratitude and duty, Jim thought. But he and Topsy had missed their dead mother always, miserable at being treated like feral foxes that Fanny had managed to trap and sought to tame.

The Baptist was winding up his spiel. "Forgive us all, blessed Lord, and give us, instead of despair, hope, instead of death, um . . . eternal life." Right on, Jim congratulated the minister, let's move right along, bring an end to this regretful treacle.

The organ squealed a last "Now and Forevermore," everyone shuffled to attention, and the funeral director wheeled Fanny down the aisle. The family reversed its steps out into the weak January sunshine, Jim supporting Topsy, now giggling maniacally. The preacher hadn't been that funny, Jim thought. Sallie, regal and quiet, Helen sniffling, both turned their heads from Topsy in disdain. Cousin Charlie and his wife swept by brother and sister like twin storm clouds and climbed into the limousine behind the hearse.

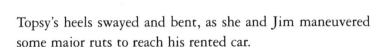

Topsy's heels swayed and bent, as she and Jim maneuvered some major ruts to reach his rented car.

She felt great, warm inside, conscious that power — over Charlie and his wife, over Sallie and Helen, even over Jim — is strength. Tomorrow, she would suffer for her behavior, for the half-distracted, wholly impersonal manner in which she was directing the disposition of her stepmother's estate. Tomorrow, she would be self-hating, turning even more to the bottle that was buffering her loneliness. If only Joe had not died; if he had been here, he would have tempered her coldness, her desire for revenge. Joe had been her only friend. She had clung to his life after the doctor said it was over. Topsy had washed the fabric of her marriage over and over again. But Jim, he discarded wives like Kleenex. Four already. And he might not be finished.

Still, playing the troublemaker after years of passiveness was a tonic. For the moment, it was pleasing to hold everyone at bay. And she had almost decided not to go near the funeral and its memories. It was only after Jim had called her from Corpus Christi that she had agreed to come.

She reached for her purse on the car's floor, and pulled out a little flask.

"Easy, sis," Jim said. "You don't want to go falling into the grave along with poor Fanny."

Topsy barked, "Screw it. What do you know? *You* try to

do two funerals in a month." She took a big swallow from the flask. Her insides glowed like the Fourth of July. Jim patted her hand. "I know, I know, it's tough about Joe . . ."

"I haveta put my grief on hold," Topsy said, enjoying Jim's concern, playing major chords on his feelings. "It isn't fair. Fanny did this to get even with me from the grave."

"Did what? She didn't plan on dyin'."

Jim doesn't know shit, Topsy thought, never did. Fanny had been the wicked stepmother of myth, driving me, her slave, before her, to wash her underwear, clean her house, endure her tongue-lashings. Lucky Jim, she ignored *him,* while Sallie, from first to last a selfish bitch, received all her praise. And what happened? Sallie deserted everybody, as if love was too rich for her constitution, while I, the former Miss Cinderella, got dragged back into the web, struggling against Fanny's assertions that she was sorry, she missed me, she needed me, I was the oldest child of her dear, dead husband, etc.

And she played me like a frenzied trout to the end. Dangled love in front of me, snatching it back time after time until death put a stop to her maneuverings. Even then, Fanny planned a careful, cruel finale, Topsy thought, clenching her fists until her long, red nails scourged her palms. Knowing full well that the cousins would resent me as a pushy coconspirator, Fanny made me the overseer of her affairs, manager of her will, guff-taker from relatives who ignored me while she lived. A nobody designated to be the overlord, an incompetent the broker of their rightful inheritance. She cursed the family for Fanny's last tantrum that had affirmed in perpetuity her stepdaughter's role of hired hand.

But it was impossible to explain to Jim her past and present inequities. It was easier to sip a little Jack Daniels.

Topsy said, "Well, it was worth coming down here just to see the look on Charlie's wife's face when the will was read, thought she was going to get everything — money, jewelry, property — hasn't she sucked up to Fanny for years, though? But this house, who's gonna buy it from me? It's a white elephant in a ghost town."

She knew, it was no secret in the family, that Fanny's house was coveted by Charlie and his wife. Charlie had never had anything good to say about the city of their childhood, Bereston was a place to escape from, but he and his wife were unbearably smug about their years of attention to Fanny's ancient furnace, peeling paint, and mysterious late-night pains.

It had been Charlie's wife who had determined that Fanny should go out in style. She had contacted the funeral director, planned the church service, and enticed the far-flung family to show up. It was Charlie's wife who had chosen the top-of-the-line, fumed oak coffin and the imposing spray of roses and gladioli, "From your loving nieces and nephews," resting on the coffin. Topsy decided not to take that slur lying down. "Still leaving us out," she said to Jim, and splurged on her own ironic floral tribute, "From your devoted children."

Topsy knew Jim would not get it. She had long ago dismissed her brother as a hopeless fool about a family who had abused and ignored them both. Jim's treatment had been no kinder than hers, but he'd endured the insults as if, like penance, they would make him stronger and wiser. Always a fool about Fanny, Topsy thought, about a woman who was wintry and controlled even when pleased. Jim never saw that Fanny, like Sallie, used him indiscriminately.

How did he hang around as long as he did, Topsy

thought, spend years between wives patching together Fanny's aging house, trying to remodel his stepmother into mellowness? Like a kid, she thought, a kid with dreams that old habits could be repaired as easily as old plumbing.

In confusion, she realized Jim was addressing her, talking a blue streak as he drove over long-abandoned railroad tracks, filling her in on last night's walk with Charlie.

"We were picking our way along the dark streets," Jim said, "when out of the blue Charlie told me that you had been encouraging him to buy Fanny's house." Topsy giggled at Jim's imitation of Charlie. "An' Topsy said this place is comin' up. My foot. Topsy's as bananas as ever, if you know what I mean. She's as raggedy as the golf course. You couldn't pay me to take Aunt Fanny's house. Spooky, that's what this place is, dead, just like her."

Jim's voice wavered as he told Topsy how he had considered pushing fat Charlie into a pothole, of which she knew there was no lack. "The houses, Tops, remember how beautiful they were with the porches all garnished with wisteria and camellias, they spelled security to me. Now they're just one after the other with black and peeling siding. Sallie's old house is a shame. I should never have left," he said sadly, and they both stared at the robin's-egg-blue limo ahead of them, bouncing over the ruts, Sallie's erect back bobbing up and down. "I could have kept up appearances."

Jim rambled on. Topsy felt he was describing a dream. "If I had ten years and gallons of paint, I would make Bereston look like Bermuda, pink and aqua and white." Topsy pictured her brother, a souped-up robot, rocketing from house to house with a paint brush in either hand, a gallon of paint slung around his neck. Poor Jim.

They were coming to the old cemetery. The cortege

turned past the privet hedges and made its way toward a green canopy and a roll of fake grass. Topsy groaned.

"You didn't tell me you asked Charlie if he wanted to buy the house," Jim said.

"Well, I sorta mentioned I'd give the family a good price. After all, those constipated nieces and nephews are gonna get money. I should know. I'm the one parceling it out to them."

Jim said, "Once the only thing I wanted in the whole world was to be part of this. Why didn't you ask me if I wanted to buy it?"

Topsy helped herself again from the flask. "You want to live in this nosy fart place, now?" She stopped, looked hard at her brother and quickly assessed his seriousness. "Okay, bro, I'll give you a good deal. You can have the mausoleum for a cut-rate price. I'm not greedy."

Then, remembering that Jim had always been long on dreams and short on cash, she fumbled at the door handle and staggered out onto the strange texture of the graveside's fake grass.

❀ ———————— ❀

The service was short so the townspeople could offer condolences. They tottered around Fanny's relatives in wonder and excitement.

Sallie avoided them by stepping over to the next plot to look at her parents' graves. The ground was thawing in the sun. Spring onions were sprouting. Sallie's heels sank into the earth. She murmured, "Let go of me, I tell you, give it up." Her parents and Aunt Fanny had never forgiven her for discarding the druggist's son and her seventh grade pupils for a vacationing alto sax player from Les Brown's Band of Renown. Philadelphia had been the first of her bolts. I was born to run, she thought, born to search for sweeter music.

Jim came over to steady her, but she shook him off. Jim was part of the problem; he belonged to a tradition where family held you so tight, you ripped away strips of flesh escaping the bonds.

She wondered if she were missed at school. This had been an exciting week, for later today the space shuttle Challenger would lift off. She had explained in chapel about Christa McAuliffe, the teacher-astronaut, exciting the girls' imaginations. She had quoted Whitman to them, "We the youthful sinewy races, / All the rest on us depend."

Homesickness impaled her. She began a conversation with a man who had been eyeing her tentatively. He looked like a Mafioso, with a moustache and snappy shades. He reminded her that his oldest brother had been in her seventh grade class so long ago. She said, "Imagine, little Jackie Rogers, with children old enough for boarding school. I'll send you some of our brochures. You can't go wrong at Malden."

Lunch was courtesy of the Methodist women. Unexplained relatives and friends wandered through Fanny's house, testing picnic fare — fried chicken, potato salad, deviled eggs, iced tea. The men popped beer tabs in the kitchen.

Helen, famished by her mourning, was sampling the five donated cakes on the dining room table. She was the youngest of the relatives, but gray-haired and shriveled. She belongs in the coffin, Jim thought, I wouldn't fuck her with Charlie's prick.

Helen put a slice of each cake onto paper plates and chewed. Crumbs rained on the lace tablecloth.

Some distant cousins were enjoying the cut glass in the china closet. "Fanny kept it all," one said. "Gems and junk."

Topsy addressed the group in a stentorian voice. This would set their teeth on edge. "See, I'm not a heir. You blood kin are. An' now you know what the paper said you were gonna get. Don't blame me for any of it. Lawyer Bledsoe's gonna deal with all the expenses and settle up. I was just supposed to tell you the story and then get out." She paused, then dug in. "Lawyer Bledsoe says I should lock up the house and its contents." The distant cousin shut the china closet door quickly.

Jim wandered into the kitchen. Charlie's wife was at the sink, an apron over her blue Ultrasuede suit, crying into two days' dirty dishes. Charlie was bending over her.

"Give up the dishes, hon. They're not yours. Let's go. Whatcha gonna learn that you haven't already?"

Charlie's wife wiped her eyes. "I want to hear the will again," she said. Then she whispered at him, "Did I miss something? Aunt Fanny didn't leave us anything special, right? Did you hear anything?" She leaned on Charlie's shoulder.

"Oh, and the last thing Fanny said to me was, 'I'm sorry. I should have changed my will.' "

Charlie patted her. "You did the right thing, anyway, you took real good care of her at the end." Charlie's wife gasped and fled, spraying Jim with the full venom of her anger.

Back at the dining table, Helen was saying, "I think the orange-mocha is the best, although the Methodist women are known all over for their Black Forest." She was down to her last slice.

"Take it with you, for God's sake," said Topsy. "Take all the cakes. There's a freezer full, too." She had eaten nothing. Helen's eyes filled with more tears.

Opening his second pack of the day, Jim retreated to the living room window, with Topsy's words trailing behind him. "Helen, if you don't stop that sniveling, I'm gonna slap you." He glanced out at the street. The warmth of the cemetery sun had dispersed. The neighboring houses, the world, were gray and bleak. Maybe snow, Jim thought. He remembered as clearly as today's news a blazing summer sun and a boy hurrying up the walk of this house, eager to escape the heat.

Behind the screen door, hidden in the shadows of the house, his stepmother had been watching for him, cool and sensual in a white, silky slip. The boy hurried, believing that at last he saw a welcoming smile. He never told anyone about that day. The illicitness of it, Fanny's bed, with the sleek cotton sheets and embroidered pillow cases, his father's girlie calendars smiling seductively from the wall, the bedroom a blur of sunshine and fright.

Remembering that boy — whose initial fear of death at the hands of his father, if not of God, gradually had given way to relief at mere accusatory coldness, as bracing as an ice cube to his forehead, from his stepmother — Jim wondered once more if he *had* been an unwitting collaborator in Fanny's fall from grace. Otherwise, why had he always played the penitent?

Jim turned away from the window. Speaking of today's

news. He flipped on the TV. It was an old black-and-white one, an original from the fifties or sixties. He remembered how he had tried to get Fanny to buy color, but she was too tight. "This one's okay with me," she had said. "I just keep the sound on for company anyway."

The blurry face of Dan Rather appeared on the tube, startling Jim. It wasn't six o'clock. He checked his watch. It was soaps time. Belle certainly seemed glued to "All My Children" or something like it at this time each day.

The anchorman's groomed features were rumpled with concern. "NASA has just announced that the seven astronauts died a few minutes ago when the space shuttle Challenger exploded in a tremendous ball of flame one minute and sixteen seconds after lift-off. On board was Christa McAuliffe, the New Hampshire schoolteacher, as well as astronaut Judith Resnik and Gregory Jarvis, a commercial engineer . . ."

Jim stood in front of the set. His country's helplessness at this moment flew out of the television like a demon and fastened to him, gibbering. In his guts, self-doubt began to grow, a cancer that dried his mouth and gnawed at his liver. He felt suddenly old and doubtful. He hardly responded when Sallie cried, "Move away, move away," and gave him a push. Like a herd of elephants leaving their feeding ground, the group in the dining room and kitchen shuffled toward the television.

Plumes of smoke erupted from the fireball on the TV screen, and the booster rockets hurtled across the sky. There was a replay of Christa McAuliffe's curly head and her gay, thumbs-up sign as she headed for the launch pad.

Sallie was mumbling incoherently.

"What?" Jim looked at her.

"This is sickening. Horrible. I've got to get back to school. The girls won't know how to deal with it." Sallie flung herself across the room and rooted about in the coat closet at the bottom of the stairs. "My coat, where is it? I've got to leave." On TV, the launch crowd was reacting. McAuliffe's parents stared at the camera, faces uncomprehending.

Some of the group in the living room turned away from the television to watch Sallie's hysterics. Helen licked her fingers of the last crumb of orange-mocha cake and snuffled.

Jim approached Sallie tentatively. He had never seen her so unstrung. Her coolness, her emotional control, had deserted her. It came to him that her girls, her charges at Malden School, were her only family now. Like a real mother, she was determined to keep her children from hurt and harm, protect them from the grimness of the world. Jim's heart ached for her. He resolved to forget his own grievances.

"I can drive you to the airport, sugar. When does your plane leave?" They struggled with the armholes of her coat. Charlie's wife appeared at the top of the stairs. She had washed and remade her face, and her eyeshadow matched her Ultrasuede suit. She adjusted her mink jacket.

"Jim, this is hardly the time for you to be pawing Sallie like that," she said, and, "Don't we have enough on our minds without all this foolishness?" The watching relatives tensed.

Jim laughed, but Sallie flared up.

"Hold your nasty tongue," she said. "You're just pissed because, with all your hypocrisy, Aunt Fanny didn't pay off."

The crowd in the living room brightened. It knew little about the Challenger. NASA was a bunch of eggheads in Houston playing with the stars. But the shuttle explosion, almost as if it had occurred in Fanny's backyard, had delivered its impact. Here was an aftermath they could understand and appreciate.

Charlie's wife flushed. "Rich man's whore," she pronounced, and stalked out the front door without another word. Sallie fled to the bathroom.

Jim went to say goodbye to Topsy. She had not moved from her place at the dining table. Now, like a stage manager, she gathered up her props — her copy of the will, her little silver flask — and arranged them in the depths of her purse.

"We're finished here," she said aloud, and dragged herself to her feet. "Jim, honey, turn off that TV and get this lot outa my house."

She paused at the dining room window, where pots of Fanny's African violets — pink, mauve, deep purple — thrust their delicate blooms and fuzzy leaves toward the weak winter light. Fanny had nurtured the exotic plants like premature infants. If you touched them, they shriveled.

Topsy plucked a violet and stuck it in Jim's buttonhole.

Then she blurted, "I don't know what we're going to do without her. We're going to miss her so much. I think she'd want me to get this house painted, don't you?" Spontaneously, she embraced her brother.

Jim hugged her back. It didn't matter that Topsy was drunk, Sallie enraged, Charlie and his wife unsettled by a turn of events they didn't deserve. Fanny, involuntarily, had managed to gather her family together one last time, forcing them to react once more, re-energize. Jim shivered in excitement. He was driving Sallie to the airport. Obediently, he went to persuade the others they all had long trips ahead of them.

A Little Lovely Dream

❋ ——————————————— ❋

*O*utside the Amber Palace, an unforgiving sun pressed like weights on the travelers' heads. Inside the marble coolness, Mr. Arun Lal, guide for Discovery Tours of India, was explaining purdah to the American group, pointing out the women's quarters of the palace. "I must be telling you very truthfully, dear sirs and madams, that behind these heavy draperies were watching the puppeteers and musicians, in the great hall below, the most indulged, beautiful women in the world."

Carrie Penny laid her cheek against a marble column and watched the albino monkeys chase each other across the parapets of the old fortress. Mr. Lal's voice, upholstered with unpredictable ascents and descents, made her giggle.

Carrie was already disappointed in the trip, even after her study of the subcontinent's culture and history. Her friends in yoga class had all been to ashrams. They said, "You'll love India. It's the place to find yourself."

She had hoped that their guide would be as dashing and

skillful as previous ones she and her husband, Fred, had employed. She remembered fondly the muscular white hunter in Kenya and the ferocious Greek skipper who had sailed them safely through high winds in the Aegean. The little group she and Fred traveled with expected not only deluxe accommodations for their American dollars, but also glamorous baby-sitters.

But Mr. Lal seemed less interested in charming his group than in educating them. "India is being the master of nuclear fission," he preached early on. "We are having parity in this regard with the capitalist west." As he finished his lecture on India's superiority, he stepped briskly over the trash piles of deformed beggars blocking their exit from the hotel.

"Please do not be giving them any baksheesh. It only encourages them," he cautioned, while the Americans shuddered. How could you ignore the stumps, the leprosy, the noses and mouths that had rotted into black holes?

After three weeks, Carrie's enthusiasm for new experiences lay exhausted by the poverty, wrapped in piercing heat, that dogged them. Sometimes she refused to leave the hotel, refused to run the gauntlet of shame. Fred said, "We've paid for this trip, let's enjoy it." He had already used up 20 rolls of film, shielding himself from everyday affronts behind his Nikon.

Fred's favorite subject was the Indian women, who seemed to flourish like the jasmine and bougainvillea amid the squalor. The group was moved by their delicate arms, draped from shoulder to wrist with bangles of ivory, silver, and glass. "Their family's entire worth they are wearing on their arms," said Mr. Lal dismissively, and Carrie wondered if they slid off a bracelet, one by one, to buy matches, some rice, a stew pan.

Jingling and tinkling, females large and small trudged along roads far from any village, bent under loads of wood or sacks of cow dung. Where were they coming from and where were they going? Their fragile saris and open sandals swept up the dust and filth.

Sometimes they took to larceny. The week before, on the way to Ranakpur, the group had stopped on a hill by a bullock-powered water wheel to take photos and picnic. Carrie had been entrusted with a bag of oranges.

Within seconds of their arrival, little girls, no more than eight or nine, tiny adults in their orange and red saris, materialized like rainbow specters behind a camel caravan toiling up the hill. The children surrounded Carrie at once, brushing their saris against her, laughing and shouting. She had learned from previous travels that Third World kids, unlike Western children, sought her out, attaching themselves to her with an instinctive sense of her vulnerability.

A small boy in ragged shorts wandered up, begging, "One rupee, one pen," while the little girls whirled around them. Carrie smiled benevolently to mask a feeling of alarm.

The rest of the group, busy getting drinks from the ice chests in the car trunks, or examining the intricacies of the water wheel, ignored the scene. Carrie was dimly aware that in the background Fred focused intently on his shots of children decorated with betrothal balls at the parting of their hair.

The girls suddenly stopped giggling and circling and leaped at Carrie and the bag of oranges. Carrie staggered, the bag fell into the dust and the oranges rolled in all directions. The children grabbed the oranges and, shrieking with laughter, darted away. But the game wasn't over. Carrie felt a movement at her side.

"One pen," yelled the boy. He danced around Carrie, clutching her gold Cross pen. "Wait a minute," she said, reaching for the child, "that's my good pen, give it back." "One pen," he yelled again, and sped off after the little girls. Their gauzy saris streamed behind them like kite tails.

Carrie sat down on a stone and dusted herself off. Her throat was worse than dry; it was scorched. She reached into her bag, where the flap had opened to reveal her gold pen to the beggar boy, and took out her plastic bottle of soda water. It was hot and tasted soapy. She applied some comforting lipstick.

Fred had moved off to photograph another aspect of the Ranakpur road, unaware of her distress. He was probably planning his India lecture to the Rotary Club, Carrie thought. The others were drinking lemon and lime Limca sodas and admiring the tiny tot driving the bullock round and round the water wheel. He was enjoying the attention and poked his stick at the animal's anus to get it to move faster.

Only Mr. Lal, who had half-heartedly cried out, "*Acha,*" at the children as they ran off, came over to Carrie and gazed out over the parched wheat fields at a mud hut in the distance. Carrie took a deep breath. She didn't need the oranges, in spite of her constant dehydration. And the pen? Tomorrow, the little boy would be the pride of his school, with a beautiful gold pen to show and tell. She communicated this thought to Mr. Lal.

"Unlikely, my dear madam," he said, pursing his lips. "The child is very likely not attending the school, and tonight his father will be taking the pen from him and selling it at the bazaar. Fetching a good price, no? The family will then be buying some rice or, perhaps, lentils, food for a month. These people are very poor."

Carrie was ashamed of her anger. Surely, keeping a family in rice for a month was more important than the kid's temporary pleasure or her selfish need. She should have brought ten Cross pens. But she found herself angry at Mr. Lal, who supposedly was her protector for the few weeks she was traveling with him. Couldn't he have anticipated the incident?

But Mr. Lal was disinclined to apologize. His injured, liquid eyes made Carrie feel she had been at fault, that by tempting the children with her unflapped purse and her bag of oranges, she had behaved improperly. From that day on, he kept giving her sidelong glances, which she interpreted as fear of further disgraceful behavior.

Lying in her hotel room, a wet washcloth on her forehead, she listened to Fred. "Don't fret about it. It wasn't your fault. The same thing could happen in the slums of the U.S." She knew this was true, that tourists must be wary, but she felt an ebbing of her will. That night she dreamed of being strangled by an albino monkey.

Now, at the Amber Palace, Carrie fanned her face and stared at Mr. Lal. Everyone was enjoying his story about a former maharaja of Amber who continued to defend his territory from attackers even after his head was cut off. Fred, her husband, president of Penny's Interiors, was laughing harder than anyone. Carrie remembered how he had resisted this trip, saying, "India is a sorry country; the people are overbearing and the food inedible."

Now, he interrupted Mr. Lal's lecture. "Good thing it was his head and not his *lingam*." At home, Fred had to maintain an attitude of probity, but here in the strange mixture of heat and eroticism, he encouraged prurient tales and searched out sexual symbols. Currently, he was reading about the phallic manifestations of Lord Shiva.

Mr. Lal was not unaware of tourists' interests. Yesterday, he had told them the tale of an eccentric former prince who ate crushed diamonds to improve his virility.

But now he blushed. "Oh, good sir," he said, "do please remember that the worship of the *lingam* is being a prayer for fertility, not being erotic. Sons are the lifeblood of India." Carrie wondered if he had any little lifebloods. He must certainly have a wife; otherwise, how did he stay so neat? He was younger than they, in his mid thirties, plump and a dandy. In the evening, he wore Italian-cut suits, with slim shoes. By day he wore *kurta* pajamas, clean and cool looking, or pleated trousers and a billowing white shirt. He was a sartorial contrast to the Americans, who strode around in Wallabees, well-worn chinos, and an assortment of sun hats.

The group clambered up to the palace's hall of mirrors, a series of small rooms covered inside and out with convex pieces of colored mirror glass set in patterns of stars, moons, and Aryan swastikas, outlined in gold and silver. A crowd of vagrant wanderers, holy men, and vacationing Indians was already there, smelling of unwashed bodies, urine, and heavy hair oils. It was a relief to retire to the palace's roof garden. A breeze blew and ruffled the lake below.

Carrie shook her wet hair from her neck and said to Mr. Lal, "There are too many people in India."

"It is being the world's largest democracy," he said, "and Planned Parenthood is being active since the 1960s."

"Doesn't seem to have made a dent." Carrie fanned her face, and wished there were a *charpoy* she could lie down on.

Below in the palace courtyard, she could hear the trumpets of the tourist elephants and the spiel of the hawkers competing for the attention of the mob.

"Please?" said Mr. Lal, "a dent means?"

"A population decrease."

Again, he looked hurt. He ran his hands through his oiled hair. "Hindu people are believing in large families, loving children. And such as here" — he threw out his hands in an expansive gesture to take in the countryside — "for help in the fields and for old age farmers need sons. You understand this?"

"With what you could save on the care and feeding of one child, you could probably buy a tractor."

"Where would a poor farmer be buying a tractor?"

Fred nudged her. "Leave the guy alone. He's just trying to do his job. Don't make it difficult for him." Not for the first time, Carrie glared at Fred. His sensible attitude was more irritating abroad than at home.

Riding back to the hotel, Carrie sat in the back of their bus and smoked a Beedie. It was the workingman's cigarette, a tiny brown leaf, rolled tightly by the small hands of child labor, smelling sweet like marijuana. Beedies were legal and cheap. Beedies and Indian beer, Carrie thought, were her keys to survival.

Happily she smoked, watching the roadside. The bus honked at camel carts, goats, and buffalo herders. An assistant up front with the driver shrieked at the human sea, his job to part it for their bus. Mr. Lal wandered back in her direction.

He said, "Pardon me, Mrs. Carrie, but you must be careful not to be taking too much sun, and surely you are finding those cigarettes too strong."

The bus lurched, and a cow that had almost been struck stared at her through the window. Carrie laughed. "Even the cows are stoned," she said. "Mr. Lal, do you have a wife?"

"Since four years," he said. "I am being a householder, with a three-year-old son and a new motorbike." Carrie noticed the red stains on his otherwise straight white teeth. He chewed betel nut. As if aware of her disapproval, Mr. Lal closed his mouth at once.

Carrie stammered, "Your wife, did you choose her yourself?" She was high, she realized, from the Beedie and the sun, and talking more than she should.

Mr. Lal looked placid. He said, "No, no, my Munja, my parents had good friends, you see, with a daughter. Mommyji found Munja exceptional, the right sort of daughter-in-law she could always be teaching and training . . . And Munja is still but a child, who is complaining of her confined life. She envies my job and is often requesting permission to accompany me to my parties with clients."

And for sure, she'll never make it, thought Carrie, conjuring up an Indian mouse scrabbling after Mr. Lal's importance. She took a final puff of the Beedie. A soft cloud of air caressed her and she lay back and floated on it.

Fred looked up from a copy of *The Times of India.*

"Are you two discussing nonviolence?" he asked.

"No, life enhancement," said Carrie, and Mr. Lal smiled politely, his hand over his mouth.

She said, "Anyhow, Mr. Lal, it seems to me that nonviolence in India is about as effective as birth control. Aren't the Sikhs and Hindus killing each other still in the Punjab, and what about Sri Lanka?"

Mr. Lal had a ready answer.

"Sad, this wanting violence," he said. "These people,

they are placing personal needs before God, before the teachings of their religion."

Carrie remembered how strongly Mr. Lal felt about his gods. When the group had visited some desert villages, little kids had stood along the wayside, eating their dust, waving and crying out, "Ta ta." Mr. Lal stopped the jeep and lectured them.

"No ta ta," he said in Hindi, "Say *Ram, Ram.*" Then he explained to his group, "They learned 'ta ta' from the British. Better to wave and say 'God, God.' "

That same day, Mr. Lal introduced her to opium. The drug was illegal and dangerous to come by in Delhi. Out in the desert, it was openly grown, poppy fields raising their white and pink flowers next to lentils and wheat. When the group stopped at one village, Mr. Lal said he would be offered opium as a gift of hospitality by the head man, and that they could do as they wished about accepting it.

The opium was passed around in little balls the consistency and color of tar, as they sat cross-legged in a cow-dung-and-urine-paved courtyard. Fred refused. So did the others, politely accepting cups of muddy tea. Carrie picked up a small piece of opium. Perhaps this was what India was all about. Mr. Lal leaned over to her and whispered, "Just be taking a small bit, please? Sometimes illness results." Then he plopped a sizable pat into his own mouth and chewed. Carrie took a tiny chunk and as it passed from point to point in her mouth, she was conscious that everything in its path numbed, like the work of Novocain. The effects on Mr. Lal, however, were more startling. On the drive home, he sang out "Ta ta" to the waving children and blew them kisses.

Later, he lectured the group on opium as a boon to the Indian peasant, more valuable than a field of wheat, how it deadened the pangs of hunger and pain, how a baby sucking some from a finger will stop crying, and how in many peasant homes it is offered as an accompaniment to tea.

"There are some advantages to being a tourist-handler," Fred said. "Maybe opium would be better for us than yogurt tablets." Carrie knew that Fred and the group disapproved of her for showing off.

In the middle of dinner, as the group was discussing the merits of yogurt tablets to prevent tourist stomach, Carrie thought fondly of the drug and the remains she had hidden in her purse. She asked Mr. Lal if he often took opium. "No, no," he protested, "only to be polite. And you, Mrs. Carrie, are being full of adventure, I think." He recited a poem in her ear, "From the poppy-bole / For you I stole / A little lovely dream."

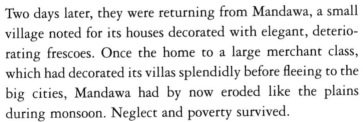

Two days later, they were returning from Mandawa, a small village noted for its houses decorated with elegant, deteriorating frescoes. Once the home to a large merchant class, which had decorated its villas splendidly before fleeing to the big cities, Mandawa had by now eroded like the plains during monsoon. Neglect and poverty survived.

Carrie drifted. Fred had left the night before to buy wicker furniture in Hong Kong, a device he used when bored with pleasure trips. The irregular Indian telephone service prohibited ready access to the home office. Carrie refused to go with him. "No work this time, you promised," she said. Fred tipped Mr. Lal and charged him to watch over her.

Stubbornly, she shuffled behind the group down the

lanes turned to muddy ditches by a heavy rain. Examining the frescoes, she held her nose against the open sewers and fly-covered market stalls. Mr. Lal clung to her anxiously.

The major spring holiday, called Holi, was in full swing. The streets were full of revelers in rags, their faces streaked blue, red, yellow, green with the dye they had thrown at each other. Even their hair was colored. They were also drinking something Mr. Lal called toddy, a fermented wine from coconut palms. They closely resembled the Sioux nation on the warpath.

Mr. Lal wished to avoid those partyers who had been up all night and were now staggering down to the village square to burn their old clothes. "This is a symbol," he said, urging the group on, "of casting off winter's gloom — or perhaps they may be celebrating Krishna's fertility." Except for a few squirts of color and some stones directed at the windshields of their cars, no incidents disturbed their departure.

Mr. Lal accompanied Carrie in her car, one of three in their motorcade, and as soon as they were into the country-side, he fell asleep. In anticipation of the three-hour trip back to Jaipur, their young driver floored the accelerator, and scattered pedestrians, bicyclists and motorbikers along the rutted two-lane roadway. Intercity buses rushed into their path, people clinging to their sides and tops. Cows wandered onto the road.

Carrie cried out at intervals, "Slow down! Watch out! Driver, do you see that cow?" The driver answered, "Yes, memsahib," and increased the pressure on the gas pedal.

She took a Beedie from her purse and tried concentrating on positive aspects of the trip — the tasty *dal*, the tandoori chicken. She hoped Fred had good photos of the fruit-salad saris, their owners weighted with nose rings and heavy silver ankle bracelets. She reminded herself to learn more about Moghul paintings and the Hindu religion.

Mr. Lal snorted in his sleep. Tires squealed, and from nowhere a bicycle reared up and crashed into the car. A bundle of rags painted Holi colors flew along the hood and into the windshield. The windshield shattered and the Australian Holden careened off the road and into the ditch.

Carrie was calm as Mr. Lal dragged her from the smoking car. Threatening-looking celebrants had already appeared on the scene, shouting aimlessly and staggering about in their dye-struck garments. Some less inebriated citizens made a litter of cloths and dragged the inert bundle off the car's hood to the local dispensary. Carrie's driver sat dazed by the side of the road. No police were in evidence.

Carrie touched a lump on her forehead.

"What happened?" she said to Mr. Lal. "Who did we hit? What should we do?"

Mr. Lal's smooth, almond face looked tired. But he took charge in a manner that suggested he had fended off many such crises. He bundled Carrie into the second car, and had a few words with Carrie's driver. He urged the remaining two cars to hurry on.

"An accident," he said, "an unfortunate accident, involving a drunken young man on a bicycle. Please do not trouble yourself, Mrs. Carrie. The police will be coming to question our driver, yes, and the company who employs him will be dealing with the consequences. Discovery Tours must be caring for its clients first and foremost."

They were all silent, remembering the surly crowd, who had witnessed one of its own gunned down. Carrie shut the consequences out of her consciousness. She felt the driver deserved his fate, but she couldn't forget the bicycle crumpled around the car's grille and bumper.

Spasms of responsibility gave Carrie a fearful headache, so they drove home very carefully.

Carrie is in her hotel room, clothes, presents, books strewn on the chairs, the floor, in the armoire. She has made no headway packing. She leaves tomorrow morning at 5 A.M. for Delhi and home, but she is flat out on the bed, an ashtray full of Beedie butts on her stomach. She has taken several Fiorinals and a Halcion. Soon, she will fall asleep amid the debris of her trip. Perhaps she will leave it all behind. There is a tap on her door. "Mrs. Carrie, is all in order?"

"Certainly," she calls out, far from sure. "Yes, I'm all right."

But the sound of her voice does not assure Mr. Lal. "May I just be briefly informing you of the arrangements for tomorrow?"

Carrie pulls her bathrobe together, and opens the door.

Mr. Lal is worried. He is facing a disheveled foreign female with the acrid smell of Beedies on her breath. And he must put her in order before he completes his final duty, seeing her safely on the plane. He says, "I am hoping that you have not been finding my country too taxing. It is so large, so undisciplined, so full of unexpected occurrences. But you must not be worrying about today. I have already been checking with the auto company. Even now, the driver is sleeping in his home. The local magistrate found him not guilty of hitting that fellow, owing to drunkenness."

Tears rise to Carrie's eyes. "But what about the bicyclist? How is he?"

Mr. Lal is vague, but assuring. "He is in hospital, no doubt resting comfortably." His concern sounds minimal, if not absent.

"In our country, we say that exploring is being delightful to anticipate, satisfactory to contemplate later, but perhaps not so comfortable at the time. And you, Mrs. Carrie, must be off tomorrow early, so perhaps you should pack a little . . ."

Carrie feels herself sliding away. "Later . . ."

As she drifts off, Mr. Lal starts to fold her belongings. He lays shirts and trousers in the bags. He sweeps the quiet room clean of her detritus. He stacks her bags neatly on the luggage racks. Then, he sits down cross-legged in a corner of the room, and by a dim light begins to read one of Carrie's books about Calcutta. It is as yet not available in India.

At one in the morning, Carrie wakes. Her headache is gone. She focuses on the tidy room, on the quiet figure reading.

"Oh, Mr. Lal," she says, "I'm really embarrassed. Did you do all this for me?"

"It is being my pleasure," he says, standing and bowing.

"I hope you are paid overtime," she says.

"No, madam, you may disbelieve what I am telling you, but in all truthfulness, I must be saying that I earn but 1,350 rupees per month, which is about 35 U.S. dollars per week."

Fleeting thoughts of Fred remind Carrie that this disclosure is not exactly professional. And what would Fred think of Mr. Lal packing her suitcase, fondling her under-wear?

She quickly changes the subject. "Do you know, Arun, what I find especially admirable about Indians? They have perseverance."

Mr. Lal leaves his dim corner and joins Carrie on the bed. He lays the book, *The City of Joy,* on the night table. "A compelling book about my country, do you agree?" he says. "And one that my Munja could be learning from. Perhaps you would be finding it possible to lend it?"

"Anything," she says hastily. "Yes, do take it — with my compliments."

He smiles at her lazily, takes her hand in his. Then he parts his large lips and kisses her gently on the mouth. His lips are sweet and his breath smells of anise. She remembers that Fred has always been a very generous tipper.

Freud Speaks

❀ ──────────────── ❀

$\mathscr{B}$uck hesitates by the bedroom door, trying to gauge her mood level. Today, he reckons it's on empty. Billie lies on the rose silk comforter, in a fetal position. A Rorschach of tears stains the fabric.

"Hi, babes, bad day, huh? Is it your manuscript again?"

Billie raises her head, wipes her eyes, looks at her husband in desperation.

"I give up, it's hopeless, I'm a failure . . ."

This is nothing new to him. He sits next to her, the down of the comforter, like her body, soft and giving to his weight.

"Everybody says this business demands a lion's share of returns. Rejection goes with the territory. It's just a matter of time . . ."

But Billie has tuned out. Buck's attempts at comfort are succeeding less and less. Love is not enough for Billie. Her babies, those short stories she conceives and coaxes into birth, emerge like premature, deformed infants. She keeps sending them out, anyway. She craves acclamation, appreciation, publication.

Buck searches for a diversion once more.

"Look what I've brought you, I need your advice."

He opens a package, places three books on the coverlet. Instead of the puddle of tears, gaudy four-color jackets stare up at Billie.

"The Pulitzer jury choices for fiction this year. Jack Green, Herb Stein and I make the final decision."

Buck fights her listlessness. Billie never watches TV, has little time for music. She sustains herself with daily bouts of creativity at the word processor. He sympathizes with her struggle, her fragile ego battling the odds. When she isn't composing, she reads hungrily, as if drawing the language into her veins. She reads Edith Wharton and Lorrie Moore, endless biographies of dead literary nabobs, and all the trade magazines. She is knowledgeable about the politics and scandal of the publishing world, a critic of the bogus and pretentious that masquerade as art.

Yet, it is Buck, the editor of a prestigious daily in their midwestern university town, who has won the prizes, the national esteem and, finally, the honor of serving on the Pulitzer advisory board. Despite the anomaly of his election to the fiction panel, he whose professional life is anchored in fact, Buck has received much acclaim for articulating his winning choices. He has also taken some ribbing about the probability of spousal coaching.

"You're so much better than I am at knowing what's hot and what's not," he says now to Billie, with full knowledge of his wife's hopelessness, but without a workable solution. "Will you read these and give me your thoughts?" The irony of this appeal, like their relationship, touches them both.

Putting aside her despair, Billie approaches the books. The first one, with a cover drawing of a tough-looking woman in buckskins, has rewritten the Old West from the Native American's point of view. Its author, a female Ogalala Sioux, is currently fashionable, but according to literary scuttlebutt needs extensive editing.

The second is a first novel, a Norse saga well received for its careful research, especially of sexual practices among the disciples of Odin and Thor. The cover drawing depicts a bear disemboweling a man, while a woman cowers in a cage.

The third, with a simple black-and-white cover, is called *Fantasy in F Major,* its author Jerome Blackburn.

Billie picks this book up and looks quizzically at Buck. "Yes," he says, "you got it. The man, himself."

Last summer, Billie and her fellow students of the university's fiction workshop had been in a frenzy of anticipation. Jerome Blackburn, celebrity writer and media darling, was scheduled to direct the workshop for two weeks.

On the first day, 15 people hunkered like blackbirds over the desks of room 12, Fine Arts building. Outside, sensible folk with less ambition frolicked at the lake or snoozed under shady trees.

Fifteen minutes late, Jerome Blackburn swept into the room. He flung his hat and jacket onto the floor, along with a pile of manuscripts, obviously theirs. Paper clips flew.

"Puerile, banal, peevish, insipid," he declaimed. "Syntax excruciating, style execrable, content boring. Let's get to work."

That was only the beginning. The class's self-esteem plummeted daily, as Blackburn tore apart language and longings.

"Shock therapy," said the more philosophical students.

"Brilliant," said the brown-nosers. The rest took to calming their nerves at a local bar.

The only student who excited the master was a Kathleen Turner blonde. In exchange for keeping quiet in class, the blonde received hearty Blackburn appreciation outside of it.

The day Billie had her personal conference with Blackburn, she quaked as she entered his office, her notebook clutched like a shield against her breast.

Blackburn took his time putting her into focus. He finally uncovered her wrinkled manuscripts beneath some empty Tylenol bottles and butt-laden coffee dregs. "Archaeological intelligence, moral outrage in an irresponsible world, fervent passion directed against macrocosmic idiocies." Billie unknit her fingers. Her work had all that?

Blackburn went on. "Your own, um, stuff, lacks vigor, energy. Woman's work. You're not hungry; it's obvious you depend too much on beauty and compassion. That's not what it's all about — these silly soft maunderings. RELEVANCE. That's the name of the game."

No rebuttal formed on Billie's pale lips. She felt ill, blasted by academic death rays. Blackburn scrabbled about the detritus and produced a tired-looking galley proof. "My new book. I lived for three months with the Shining Path, did you know that? Mud, dysentery, death, *comprende?* I sold myself to the slave master of drugs and lust. Out of that came brilliance. *Es necesario, es necesario* — to be a good writer, you must have balls!"

Blackburn's passion rose in direct proportion to his consideration of his own work. He seemed to have forgotten the nature of the conference. Exiting his office, Billie barely managed to make it to the bar where, three hours later, Buck found her soddenly lecturing a textbook salesman on achieving spiritual growth by connecting with a higher source, like St. Theresa or Elvis.

At the workshop's end, Blackburn left his students in a roar, waving from Kathleen Turner's little Alpha. For six months, Billie's word processor was silent. Only gradually did she return to her stories of innocence lost.

Now, Buck takes her hand and lifts it to his lips. He says, "Don't waste your time on *Fantasy in F Major*. I read about 20 pages, and didn't understand a thing. Blackburn must've been stoned when he wrote it, so I convinced Jack and Herb that it's incomprehensible. Somebody needs to rein that guy in. But give me your opinion on the other two. Your help means a lot to me."

In the silence that follows, Buck thinks, "The bastard, he deserves to die." He hugs his unresisting wife, then departs for the bathroom, singing cheerfully, "The old gray stud, he ain't what he used to be."

Billie looks at the three books lying on the comforter. Her husband believes he has lifted her spirits. He has played the parfit, gentil knight, riding out on his charger to do battle, protecting his lady fair. But, without knowing it, Buck has made a joke of Freud's maxim that "anatomy is destiny". *Her* anatomy will drive *Blackburn's* destiny, not her own.

She throws the three books across the room. Two of them she will never touch. The third, when Buck is gone, she will circle cautiously, tentatively. She will stare at *Fantasy in F Major* as if it is a mirage, an oasis that exists only in her tortured, desert-parched mind. But she will overcome her apprehensions and embrace the book in frazzled disbelief. She will open it with care, note the publisher, sneer at the self-serving blurbs and the portrait of the author on the jacket cover, suave but with a hint of decadence. Was the photo airbrushed? Billie remembers Blackburn with jowls, his face plowed from nostril to mouth with furrows.

Finally, crawling gratefully to page one, she will plunge facedown into the novel, drink in with humility its easy imagery, skillful narrative, spellbinding certainty. She will not put down *Fantasy in F Major* until, like an opiate-drenched lake, Blackburn's work has sedated her pain-wracked spirit.

But her husband must never know of this; she must manufacture considerations on the other two novels while hiding *Fantasy in F Major* from his sight. From now on, Billie and Buck must lie to each other about his sincerity, his appraisal of Blackburn's novel as a literary misfire undeserving of prizes or even consideration. Worse, they must also pretend that Billie's sufferings have been purified, that the careful, cold dash of love's revenge has extinguished forever the burning coals of envy.

Social Security

❀ ──────────────────── ❀

*T*he dinner party is proceeding as planned; all the guests are comfortably drunk. Swells of laughter rise and fall around the table, and I know it is going to be another of Gwen and Arthur's fabulous evenings. Two wines and champagne, Elegant Eats' A-list menu and the service of Inez and her staff always raise the impeccable to the ineffable. Gwen is my favorite hostess; she exists to produce the award-winning show.

Not that she need concern herself tonight. There is not an anchorman or current cabinet member among the guests. Instead, the chairman of Sovern Pharmaceuticals, International, and his brilliant, beautiful wife are entertaining the hard-working top management of Arthur's drug company and their spouses. The guests may not be up to Gwen's table or Arthur's vintages but, as they lower their servile shanks beneath the very same Sheraton that has upheld the elbows of Elizabeth Taylor *and* the president of the United States, they can feel the aura.

Arthur, the genius of Sovern PI, is the last gasp of an old New York family, raised on German governesses and special occasions at the Tip Toe Inn. He rescued a sleepy Yonkers drug business, going to seed after its one success with a cure for yellow fever, and turned it into Sovern PI, bigger than Sterling Drug and more astute than Robins. In the last ten years, Sovern has produced a coated aspirin and SP-327, a cataract cure. On the verge of a major breakthrough — a day-after pregnancy-prevention patch — Sovern is today the envy of the drug industry.

At Sovern's headquarters, Arthur Sovern rules with a benevolent but iron hand. *Fortune* has called him a decisive manager with clear goals, leading one of the five most respected companies in the U.S. And no detail escapes his eye, from the graphics in the annual report to once securing the freedom of a chemist in the Gulag.

His philosophy of management has always been paternal, congenial. He and Gwen entertain company execs often, imagining the underlings regard such occasions as delightful perks of the job. None tells him different.

For these command performances, Sovern management hustles its anxious wives into their Loehmann's designer dresses. Cadillac Sevilles cross the bridges and tunnels, arriving in the neighborhood of Fifth and 75th by 7:15. After circling the block six times, the Caddies deposit the discounted Victor Costas under the canopy of the Sovern's co-op promptly at 7:30. Like tourists in the Vatican, the group spends the evening in awesome wonder — at the doorman who points imperiously toward the walnut-paneled elevator, at the tailcoated uniform of the elevator operator, at the arrival on floor 16, door opening silently into the Sovern's foyer, glossy black with one tiny Chagall artfully spotlighted.

At 11 P.M., the Sevilles will be fetched from a nearby garage, suffering only minor scratches from their encounters with the parking gorillas. They will plunge recklessly up the FDR Drive, as relieved as their inhabitants, who are loosening ties and girdles, relaxing with Easy Listening on WPAT.

Nonetheless, a dinner invitation from the chairman demands outward nonchalance. I know the drill; I once dealt with it myself. It's essential to mask that fluttering in the gut that signals — what? — the fear of being branded a social inept, so dazzled by the line of flat silver marching away on each side of the service plate, or by the glamorous hostess, that sweat trickles slowly along the Brooks Brothers shirts and the silken party dresses. Accordingly, the conversational level is cautious at first, the guests as tongue-tied as children brought for the first time before adults.

In this rarefied world, the backbone of successful dinner parties is funny, vicious gossip, a commodity not traded well intracompany. Somehow, on Fifth Avenue, talk of breeding Scotties and tomatoes does not energize as it might in Short Hills and Pelham. This is where I come in.

I am not exactly the court jester, more the company magician. Officially Gwen's dress designer, I'm the flashy dahlia in a bed of sedate Peace roses. "Ezra," says Arthur, "that's the most colorful dinner jacket I've ever encountered. Does it light up?"

I count myself an essential spoke in Sovern's corporate wheel, although Arthur prefers that I limit my conversation to my specialty, designer creations. "Ezra," he says, "a peacock is only exotic until it opens its mouth." It's true I can't discuss drug salesmen in Jakarta or the politics of cancer cures, but, with my mouth stuffed with pâté, I can bring back a dinner party from the edge of destruction.

Not only am I a dependable extra man, but I know how to calm those gut flutters. I trade in harmless, titillating fantasy. What Nancy B. said to Pat K. about why short, fat men make good lovers. Or K.W.'s latest PLO pal, for whom she left the Israeli general. I may read it in the gossip columns like everyone else, but from my mouth, it sounds authentic. Amusing, how easy it is to acquire authority.

"Consider yourself Conrad's Marlow, darling," Gwen says to me over preguest aperitifs, as smoothly as if she and the classics were lifetime buddies. "Only not as long-winded. Tell Ellen Callis one of those delicious fashion tales of yours, about your trip to Santo Domingo with Oscar or Issey's prediction about shoulder pads. She may be too plump for your stuff, but her daughter married to the Drexel partner isn't."

Or, "Lay that southern charm on tonight. Most of these people have never even heard of a bisexual." And neither had she, 15 years ago.

Arthur never gives me any direction. We've known each other for years, and by now he assumes I understand my role. But he's wearing me out with these evenings. Didn't he entertain this same crew just two months ago? Why is it necessary to keep up the charade, pretend that company dinners are enjoyable for everyone, when they rumble with the explosive mixture of duty and fear? It seems to me Arthur is inviting revolution in the ranks.

Even now, though the party is running itself, I see Gwen cast a critical eye over her table. Is any small thing intruding on the fairy tale? The inlaid Sheraton gleams with age and polish, the silver and china recall the Sovern wealth, and Inez and the flowers represent Gwen's own excellent management. At the opposite end, Arthur Sovern presides, his handsome, tanned face mirroring the table's glow.

Unlike the other guests, I can enjoy the scene — its hermetic bubble of beauty and grace, its microcosm of a world that goes no further than the bronze and wrought iron doors of the apartment building. Outside, all is ugliness — poverty, squalor, incompetence — but inside all is serene, well ordered. I take every chance to inhale such elegance, because beauty has always been my savior. Gwen's presence alone is total physiopleasure — as seductive as the ministrations of a competent masseur, the stroke of a lover.

Arthur and I both bask in the sunshine of our creation, feeling we hold shares in what I call Gwen Sovern Preferred Stock, and we guard our stake jealously. Gwen has far exceeded the Dow Jones averages in the years I've known her.

Twelve years ago, when Arthur was getting on, bored with being the most eligible single man in the city, he came across Gwen in a Brooklyn realtor's office, where he had gone to inquire about a piece of property for a new factory. He loved a challenge, a chance to gamble on future potential. Gwen, in spite of poor speech and a bad complexion, persuaded Arthur that her real estate was made for Sovern's needs. Shortly, she managed the more difficult task of convincing Arthur she was made for him. In record time, he married her, and moved her across the river to Manhattan. It was as far away from Flatbush as Katmandu, but Gwen had always longed to travel.

Arthur, it seemed, was incapable of error. While the eligible women in the East 70s gnashed their teeth, he went to work on his new wife as if he were the supplier and she a million-dollar client. Immediately, he turned her over to the best handlers. I was one. "I want you to give her a distinctive style," he said to me over the phone. "One that is uniquely hers, something you've never done before, that will stop traffic."

He never appeared with his wife in my salon; real men feared that if they ever stepped over the threshold of such a place, it might lower their testosterone level. But he trusted me and my style. And I was frankly thrilled to have been chosen. "Ezra, she's my wife, an affirmation of my taste, my judgment. She must be noticed, photographed. I'm giving you carte blanche, but if you don't make Gwen's wardrobe the talk of the town in six months, it's off with your head."

Soon, he was showing her off like a champion Afghan, taking her to tea with sheikhs and shakers. This was after I took over both her clothes and her glottal stops. With my help, she learned to modulate her Krajec consonants into the soft, alto molasses of my own proud state of Virginia. Today, Gwen's articulation is eastern prep, with a hint of the southland. Liz Smith has reported that Gwen's from an old Brooklyn Heights family, related to the Faisons and the Thayers, with cousins in Petersburg. Who would guess that her larynx is rooted in Eastern Parkway?

In the beginning, she had a few doubts not confessed to Arthur. So much to learn, so little time to learn it. If she'd ever read Shaw, she would have seen the resemblance to Miss Doolittle, and perhaps made unfavorable comparisons. But she didn't read, had to be weaned away from *People* magazine and the *Real Estate Reporter*. And as we marveled at her youth and freshness, she made us all eager and energetic. With us as guides, Gwen learned to shuck her natural speech along with her timidity about upper-class manners and reading tastes. She developed interests apart from storming the gates of

Studio 54. She was 25 years old and a romantic, thrilled to leave Brooklyn's gray streets. Arthur and I were 40 and welcomed the challenge.

Like the blue chip Gwen is, she's demonstrating quality right now by giving her full attention to Lance Becker, Arthur's vice president for sales. The pride of Sovern management, Lance is loyal down to his wing-tipped toes, and so hyper he could sell fridges in the Arctic Circle. His values were formed as a young Marine. You remember the graffiti: "Join the Marines, travel to exotic, distant lands, meet exciting, unusual people. And kill them." Arthur says to me, "Ezra, dress designers are as disposable as douches, but not aggressive, energetic salesmen."

One must always struggle to intuit Arthur's priorities, but I am more puzzled than normal tonight. At the moment, he seems to be trying to charm Elaine Becker, Lance's wife, out of her black pumps. Like Gwen, he is a master at making the help feel important, indispensable. He knows that a happy employee needs a stable home life, so he gives spouses full credit when they assume their share of the corporate load. Elaine, in the place of honor on Arthur's right, as loyal to her husband of 30 years as Lance is to Sovern's products, seems somewhat distracted, as who wouldn't be when the chief is staring intently into her eyes. I wonder what subject he is trying to introduce, a difficult task considering Elaine's total obsession with her grandchildren and Lance's service to Sovern, PI. I wonder if she will shortly whip out photos demonstrating the Beckers' fecundity. Arthur is putting it on a little thick, though; his left hand is patting hers. From time to time, perhaps aware of the seeming intimacy, Elaine casts anxious glances at Lance, as if afraid he will disappear.

Lance is oblivious to Elaine's unease; like a gray-haired

rooster, he preens that his wife is the beneficiary of her host's attention. Besides, Lance now is talking to Jack Stone, the chief financial officer, about more serious things — like the advantages of a nine iron over a seven when in a bad lie. The two men are talking across Kay Jones, director of personnel, who was once Arthur's secretary. Kay hates golf as much as she loves Arthur. Though I call the game postindustrial jousting, Kay says it's a sport in which the threshold of boredom is too low and the number of liars too high. There's some bitterness in her sarcasm, for even with Gwen and Arthur's clout, Kay is still on the waiting list at their golf club. Continents of drugs get sold on the fairways of the world. Even I learned to play the game.

But Kay is smiling with every one of her newly capped teeth, handsome in her Ezra Byrd design, discounted for friends like her, and she is dealing with being out of the golfing loop as she copes with other, less subtle, discrimination. She knows that neither Jack nor Lance is comfortable around her; they're too old to consider her an equal. First of all, she's a woman — spell that M-O-T-H-E-R or W-I-F-E. Not only that, but she is a colleague who is black and forthright. They think her sport, jogging, contributes as little to corporate status as membership in the bowling all-stars. She confessed as much to me when she first entered my salon looking to scrap her sensible suits for made-to-order.

"At least I can dress well, if you'll help me," she said. "At business school, they impressed on us that you must have the right tools for the job." Kay's ambition rises like waves tonight from the sleek, feline cap of her head. But she'll never be part of line management, unfortunately, unless she changes her color *and* her sex. Thus, Kay's power, vis-à-vis Sovern, is considerably less than Gwen's. So much for the reality of equal opportunity. The same could be said to apply to me. Kay and I are by far the cleverest here tonight, but we know that we must exercise our power discreetly, diplomatically, if we are to survive.

Now, Gwen is directing the brilliant sun of her attention at Percy Potter, corporation counsel and old Princeton chum of Arthur's. He is talking alimony payments. Percy is paying out to three, about to be four, ex-wives, if the little bimbo offering her platter of ripe mammaries to the pop-eyed gaze of the vice president for product development can be trusted. She confessed hopeful marriage plans to me while being fitted for the silver strapless she's wearing.

Percy fulminates about divorce lawyers. Gwen's attentive posture, I can sense, is masking a drift into her own thoughts. I've studied her so carefully for so many years that sometimes she's like an exotic species I have under my microscope. I decide she must be concentrating on the little speech she will give later.

"Think you're ever gonna match the boss's two under par?" Jack Stone is complimenting Arthur's golf game, as effortless as his management skills. Lance refuses to rise to the bait. He is, I know, I can see it in his confident slouch, off in space, orbiting in the same system as Arthur Sovern. "Arthur's the smartest guy I've ever known," he replies without a trace of envy, and with just enough volume to be heard at the end of the table. "On the golf course, in the boardroom, he's sharp. I love it in a deal when he sits so quiet and lets everybody wrangle, and then he really kicks ass, so that even those bozo investment bankers sit up."

"Yeh, and he uses the same technique when he gets you on the Buck Hill course," Jack says, looking down the table for Arthur to approve *his* wit.

Arthur diplomatically ignores them both, still concentrating on Elaine Becker. What can he be telling her that is so riveting? Arthur has never been known to spend more than the minimum amount of polite attention on spouses. Usually, he immediately involves his end of the table in a general conversation. Elaine, as if hypnotized, keeps picking up her wine glass and putting it down again, untouched.

Jack Stone turns back to Lance, crestfallen. If those geeks knew how little Arthur regards them apart from their contributions to Sovern, they'd hang themselves from the weeping cherry next to the ninth hole. I've been with Arthur when he's tired and drunk and a little mean. Then he calls Jack his numbers cruncher, his three-pen man, referring to the accountant's plastic, breast-pocket paraphernalia. He considers Lance a pitiful social climber. When Lance's daughter married some remote cousin of the Philadelphia Biddles, Lance went into debt for the wedding, and left his just-purchased copy of the *Social Register* on the piano during the reception. Arthur told me, laughing, that he copped the book and threw it out with the garbage. "Old Lance will never spend a hundred bucks for another one. Silly ass-kisser." Arthur can confess his honest emotions to me, secure that we understand each other's snobbery without fear of threat. But he also reminds me over and over that Lance is indispensable to the company. "He's the fastest rat in the entire race," is the way Arthur delicately puts it.

Now, Jack Stone, every 225-pound, red-faced inch of him, is becoming unmanageable. "Didya hear about the San Diego deal that Sid *Con*able and *Dom*inick La Conza are putting through? They're calling it the *Condom* affair." Arthur frowns. Jack's affection for the grape too often unleashes his basic crudeness, and he'll be taking some serious shit tomorrow. Arthur has as low a tolerance for locker-room talk, especially at mixed gatherings, as he does for intraoffice flirtations. But after ensuring that Jack felt his silent reprimand, Arthur turns back to Elaine with enthusiasm. Again, I wonder about the point of this evening.

The woman on Arthur's left, Arlene Stone, the accountant's wife, has received so little of her host's attention that her face matches her name. A hard Granny Smith apple, with her portly figure and green dress. Quick: Ezra to the rescue with a tale of the bulimic film star who passed out during a fitting and was flown immediately in her personal jet to the Betty Ford Clinic. I laugh. "She claims it was the bill I was about to present that did it."

Not completely sure she understands me, my dinner partner simpers. "Of course, being brought up in Portland, my Maine roots wilt at the price of designer clothes these days. They're really not made the way they used to be, are they, like Mainbocher or Dior?"

As if she or any of those lobster suckers ever saw a Mainbocher outside of a museum. And before I'd let you into my pearl gray salon, my fat friend, you must first lose 50 pounds. But still, perhaps I *should* consider a line for larger women.

"Dear Miz Stone," I say, laying on Richmond thick as sugar on a doughnut, "why, you'd be a perfect vision in my leather jumpsuit with the poly epaulets." Not too subtle; Arlene Stone pouts. I capitulate a bit. "And my seamstresses. They're the Hong Kong descendants of Miss Ellen, my sainted mother's lifelong dressmaker."

My other dinner partner, the wife of the product engineer, invades the tête-à-tête. Properly, her turn for my full attention does not come until the entrée. "Dear Ezra," she says, caressing my sleeve, although we haven't laid eyes on each other before tonight, "I must tell my daughter, the one who works for Arthur Andersen, that she owes it to herself to visit you. She often travels to Cincinnati and Cleveland, and needs a snappy corporate wardrobe." I beam my gratitude. One must take one's bouquets from any claque, no matter how unrefined.

Fortunately, I'm saved by the soup course — cream of winter melon with walnuts — which is absolute heaven, so I concentrate on my plate at last, and leave my dinner partners to do likewise. Gwen, I notice, has swum out of her reverie somewhat, inclining her graceful head once more toward Lance. I never get tired of looking at her; I believe she's at her ultimate best tonight. An autumn vision in my latest creation, a color-field dinner dress with postmodern lace panels. The orange and gold tones lend a warmth to her pale skin and glossy black hair that makes me think of Modigliani.

From the first day Gwen walked into my shop, full checkbook at the ready, we were meant for each other — I as confidante, she as a superb marketer of my designs. I was a bit outré even for New York then, but with Arthur and Gwen's support, smart women began to flock my way.

As Gwen and I got comfortable with each other, she trying on new lines, me working hard at the governess-companion role, she would sometimes say, a little pale and shaky from standing so long, "Do you think I can do this, Ezra, with my background? I want to please Arthur in every way, he's so good to me. But hey, I only had two years at Hunter. My father was a slave at the Board of Ed. When he died, I only looked as far as a house in Lawrence and a couple of kids."

I reassured her. Wasn't it my job? I was born to be

cosseted by wealth and charm. When she obsessed, "Won't people know right away I'm bogus? I don't know if I'm up for a new me," I lectured.

"Darling," I said, "we may be teaching you a few simple basics, like smart dressing and how to speak. We may teach you it's important to wear your nails short, your hair long, and never to drink from your finger bowl. But don't forget you're a Brooklyn girl, from the heartbeat of America. The Dodgers, Streisand, Coney Island. That's *your* background, tough, streetwise. Nothing will *ever* stand in your way."

"I never knew the way would wind like this," she would say, reminding me of Little Orphan Annie, fingering the silks and damasks, standing erect in her new, proud way, a queen even in her underwear. She learned so fast, even I almost forgot what she used to be. And she was grateful. "Ezra, promise you'll always be my best friend," she said when, like Eliza at the ball, she had had a particularly spectacular evening.

Even temporary problems like her skin, which had at first showed remnants of teenage craters, were charmed into forgiveness. The old dermatologist I sent Gwen to transformed her face to alabaster in six months. Soon, she was selling more Sovern products than Lance Becker's entire sales staff. As I began to see her serene countenance appear on Sovern products — skin abrasives, acne removers — I took the opportunity to buy stock in the company. It could only go higher.

And Arthur understood how well his long shot was running the race. He was used to success, as slick a salesman of himself as he was of his products, but he was as proud of Gwen as I. Sovern Pharmaceuticals gave birth to more products, at home and abroad. Whenever Gwen dedicated a factory or appeared at a drug convention, Sovern's stock rose in wild applause.

I was lucky enough to hitch a ride on the magic kilim of this daughter of destiny, even as I understood the travel costs. No matter how co-opted by luxury and grandeur, I never relinquished my right to criticize and comment, both to Arthur and Gwen. I admired them, was flattered by their interest.

I notice now that Arthur's handsome profile is still bent toward Elaine Becker. Arthur can't be discussing nineteenth-century majolica or surrealism, two of his specialties, because she couldn't pronounce the former and is entirely ignorant of the latter. And I'm still astounded at Arthur breaking another of his cardinal rules, that no spouse receives special attention. His other dinner partner, the overweight Mrs. Stone, is apoplectic.

I rescue her again as Inez removes the soup plates, giving me a little pinch while she does it. We're both Virginians, both in the Soverns' debt. I mention pointedly to my fat neighbor that Gwen is wearing one of my numbers. We both look down the table at our hostess, and I almost sigh out loud. If only one day I could have the seat of honor next to Gwen, be the recipient of her glorious smile, her quick wit, instead of having to make my magic with the crones. The plump chicken to my left reads my mind. "Doesn't Gwen look glorious tonight?" I know she is pea green, rationalizing that with Arthur's money and position, anyone could be as spectacular. Wrong, wrong, wrong: Arthur did teach Gwen a lot, but her talent to enthrall is her own special art, and that's what captivated Arthur in the first place. Very deliberately, he picked her out of the crowd, instinctively recognizing a princess among the peasants.

By now, Gwen has been photographed endlessly; no charity benefit could succeed without her. She runs all her interests — appearance, marriage, charities — with the efficiency of a nuclear submariner. She no longer has to pause before she speaks, edit her errant thoughts or shaky grammar. Now she speaks out on everything from politics to poker with an assurance that seems genetic. I reckon Arthur considers his marriage fully as successful as his company; he's said so a million times, in wonder, as if he had discovered that Gwen was another of Sovern's products, a rare combination of various chemicals that could change the sociology of the country.

And with the exception of an old sweetie hidden in a Boca Raton condo, Arthur has played a dutiful Nick to Gwen's Nora. Arthur has always been responsible about his duties to the company, to his late mother, to his various amours. I admire him for that; it's the way we were taught that a gentleman behaves. Not like today's young men, inseminating carelessly and then, like hounds, off immediately after the next scent. Never complain, never explain, is Arthur's motto, coupled with a proud arrogance before which criticism is stillborn. I don't think Gwen knows about Arthur's lady friend; Arthur is discreet, and Gwen's role of Number One Corporate Wife demands total concentration. I expect it is this dedication to duty that has prevented time out for children.

And I would certainly never jeopardize my position by confiding to Gwen Arthur's small sport. I like those big monthly checks from Sovern PI. I would bet my entire year's line that Arthur's Boca condo is not even extracurricular fun anymore; it's more like honoring an old debt. Arthur has said in admiration, "Gwen could give lessons in intelligence and grace to any woman I've ever known."

Only once in recent memory has Gwen complained to me, even though I always probe for the tiniest bit of doubt, in case I need to bring in reinforcements. We were having a cozy lunch about a year ago, when over the raspberries, she said, "We were both tired, of course, or he would never have said such a thing. But what Arthur said last night was, 'You may be dressed by Ezra Byrd, my dear, and a small wonder in your own right, but I hope you won't ignore Pygmalion and his pocketbook.' I went right away to my literary biography and checked out Pygmalion. Am I nothing more than that Galatea, Ezra, created to prove a point?"

I reassured her, of course, part of my charm is calming the restless natives. I told her Arthur valued her not only for what she had become, but for her real, unspoiled self. And I appealed to her pragmatism. "You wanted a bigger world than Lawrence, Long Island," I said. "Admit it. And you got devotion in the bargain. Arthur admires you beyond all others." I rattled on about her God-given talents, her noble instincts, the whole reinforcement presentation that had become as natural to me as breathing. I believed what I said, even though I noticed I had substituted the word *devotion* for *love*. Later, I wondered why I did that.

Maybe I had a momentary hesitation about the future, what would happen if Gwen tired of the big time, decided to have children and become a den mother. But Gwen seemed to accept my analysis of her business skills and changed the subject, leaving me to ponder if Arthur was being as careful with her feelings after 12 years as he had been when she was a novitiate. Would my self-serving advice get us both in trouble? I needed to bring up this delicate subject with Arthur.

I'm thinking I haven't had a chance to chat with Arthur in a while, when the main course arrives. Medallions of lamb prettily arranged on a fan of braised endive, tiny string potatoes, and caramelized carrots, brushed lightly with an orange sauce.

Lance spews out little flecks of sauce in earnest exhortation. He is comparing his home in Mountain Lakes, New Jersey, to the Garden of Eden. "I live in a place where they collect the garbage at least as often as the taxes." Then he recollects where he is, that the boss likes living in Sodom, and looks sheepish. But Gwen has learned from Arthur the secret of noblesse oblige; you adapt to Sovern people and their banality, and accept them, even give them some encouragement, exactly as you would your favorite, not-too-bright child. She is listening seriously to Lance's blather, her face benign, with a hint of amusement. I know she can't be listening. Perhaps she is secretly admiring his sturdy, muscular body. I think he pumps iron.

I'm arranging in my mind how to approach Lance on the subject of pectorals; his are large enough to challenge Schwarzenegger's. Really, if he kept his mouth shut for five minutes, I could really get off on his tough bod. Percy Potter is not so amiable. Lance is giving him the word on a 20-year-old Bergman film, *Scenes from a Marriage,* which has finally penetrated Mountain Lakes consciousness via videocassette.

"I didn't relate to it at all," Lance says. "What a cock-eyed marriage. They didn't talk to each other. Marriage is bound to fail for such selfish jackasses." What a hypocrite. I wonder if he gives Elaine Becker a single, kind thought once he jumps off her.

Percy's normal Scotch-brightened face glows even redder in anger, as he hears the implication of his own failed nuptials. And Gwen's diplomatic skills snap to attention again, as she attempts to defuse Lance. "Yes, indeed, marriage is a serious business. Arthur often reminds me that wives are stubborn, whereas husbands are resolute."

The laughter is general, but the rules of the game seem to be changing. Gwen is expending more energy than she should on Lance; like Arthur with Elaine, she is diluting her social skills unnecessarily. Lance's prejudices are as solid as pinballs. "The lack of moral fiber in our society has infected us all. Everybody is irresponsible; look at us, reeking with herpes, AIDS, and what is this stuff called crack? I'd kill any person I found giving my kids drugs."

"With a nine iron or a seven, Lance?" Jack Stone responds, looking around the table for approval. I take a stiff slug of the Mouton Rothschild.

As Kay Jones rises to the defense of a joint being ultimately less deadly than a fifth of Old Grand Dad, I notice Elaine Becker leaving the table abruptly. Arthur is shuffling with the wrong deck, completely out of character, I think. He would no more jeopardize his reputation by putting his hand on Elaine's knee than he would oppose the pro-lifers by importing RU 486. If Arthur practiced in-house lechery, Kay Jones wouldn't be director of personnel; she'd also be set up in a sunny Boca condo.

"Is something wrong with Elaine?" Lance makes a gesture at his wife's retreating back.

"Don't worry, this has been a moving evening, and she's moving out of range of your jokes," I answer. He gives me a look that says, Crawl away, slug, why does Arthur have you about, anyway? I guess I'll never get a chance at those pecs. And Lance would be so undemanding, so simple in his tastes. Funny how I can lust after him, brain- and humor-impaired though he is, yet find admirable Arthur sexually incompatible. It must be that with Lance, what you see is what you get. A no-brain, gregarious, gorgeous hunk. With Arthur, one must always be on guard, be alert for a first strike.

Lance returns to tales of battle at Pebble Beach and St. Andrews. He is boring us all beyond death.

Unfazed by the confusion, Arthur is finally concentrating his charm on the overweight Arlene Stone, who has forgotten her aggrievement and is drooling over his shirt. We are served dessert — apple pan dowdy with pecan crust and crème fraîche — when Elaine Becker slips back into her seat. She is composed, but her face is ashen. If this were any table but Arthur's, I would lay it on the fish course.

Gwen gives Elaine a puzzled glance, the first all evening, tinkles her wine glass and stands. I love the way she addresses us, slim, erect, my gown like a diamond accessory to a duchess.

"I would like to offer a toast to Sovern PI," she begins, "and to all of you here tonight. Your spirit and skill have strengthened the company and helped make it a major force in serving the growing health needs of our society. And, not so incidentally, the interests of our shareholders as well. To management and their spouses, who made it possible," she continues. "Arthur and I are forever grateful."

A professional could not have done better, set the right tone of sincerity without a hint of ooze. There is a round of polite, modest applause. Gwen smiles at Arthur as if he's judging the Academy Awards and she's a nominee. His smooth face arranges itself into a congratulatory smile, and he nods. "Thank you, my dear, and may I say we all are in your debt as well. Gracious, glamorous hostess and cogent adviser." He raises his glass. "To my wife, and to Sovern PI, two constants in this ever-changing world."

Excited buzzing, everyone high on complimentary

phrases and vintage wines. Even Kay Jones has turned amiable, not flinching when Jack Stone advises her to buy a set of clubs. "I'll look into your candidacy at Winged Foot," he says. "Give up that stupid jogging. One of these days you're sure to get mugged, if you don't ruin your reproductive organs first!" Kay manages a decent smile. Am I the only one who notices that something is amiss? Inez is removing Elaine Becker's full plate of apple pan dowdy, giving me the eye.

I wonder if I am so clever after all, if I have lost my touch. There are energies floating around this room right now that I can't access, some information of which I'm ignorant. The air in the dining room is suddenly stale, and I feel the BTU's of the bodies and the 12 candles glimmering in the George III candelabra.

"Isn't it coffee time?" I interrupt Jack Stone in midsentence. Elaine Becker is staring at the tablecloth, tears rising in her eyes, neglected by her host at last. She alone seems grateful for my rudeness and, like a sleepwalker, stands and moves toward the salon. Everyone else reluctantly rises, too, and drifts after her. I remain seated, perhaps to enjoy my Ezra Byrd masterpiece rise from her hostess position and waft across the dining room floor.

Lance, ever the polite brown-noser, grabs Gwen's chair with a flourish. She stands gracefully, and I check for any wrinkling of my new woven fabric. As Lance stands aside to let Gwen pass, his hand sweeps her arm. At his touch, she pauses in place, her face, as she glances at him, flipping its switch. Swept aside is the practiced serenity of the confident hostess, the perfect balance of caution and self-assurance. Instead, Gwen's perfect features disfigure with desire, erupt into a raw mass of longing. The blip of this involuntary impairment is so powerful it sends a blow to my stomach that echoes in my groin. I'm afraid to look around. The moment passes; quickly, Gwen refits her amiable smile, and glides away from Lance, perfection undisturbed.

He makes a little business about putting the chairs back in place, giving a blush time to recede. My knees shake in terror. Am I the only one who peeped through the keyhole? Did I see correctly? Interpret correctly? Gwen's piece of business was not the measured response of the perfect spouse, the consummate hostess. In that nanosecond, Gwen vomited up her helplessness, a patient sick with love.

Unguarded and vulnerable, Gwen has revealed not a momentary lapse or a request for a small flirtation, but a serious obsession with the star salesman of Sovern Pharmaceuticals. And one that is not new, either, but has had a chance to grow and bloom. Gwen? A love affair with Lance Becker? What madness is this? And how is it that I missed the signals, the signs, how could Gwen have lied to me so easily? I thought I knew her heartbeats. Is it poetic justice that I, Ezra Byrd, adviser, confidante, clairvoyant watchman, have been the first to sniff a merger as doomed as the black widow spider's? Gwen has outwitted us all, has kept us as ignorant of Lance as she has of her life before Sovern. I feel like a bodyguard who has lost the body, a midwife who has brought forth a hideously deformed thing.

Rage rises in my throat as I think of Gwen's risk taking. What drove her to play odds so appallingly high? Then I remember Lance's body, how I myself had admired it, how appealingly uncomplicated I judged him, a perpetual adolescent with a million enthusiasms, all painted in colors of the same bold hue. Gwen saw all that, too, and made Lance the escape hatch from Sovern's production line.

I'm afraid to look at Arthur. He is in the doorway to the

salon — his usual position for ushering the guests into their postprandial cocoon of coffee and liqueurs — following graceful Gwen as carefully as I. Behind him, in the Venturi-green salon, the guests mill about, now more relaxed and bold. They flutter over the Dalis and Miros, exclaim at the galactic glitter of Central Park West.

Arthur smiles at Gwen as they meet in the doorway. In his facial expression — is there pleasure, favor, jealousy? I watch to see if he will gather her up and fly, like two heavenly hosts, over the heads of us mortals. Or will they, like thoroughbreds, prance proudly into the salon?

Inez and her help circulate with the silver coffeepots and tiny espresso cups. Only Elaine Becker, on an ottoman near the fireplace, refuses. She is blowing her nose as Lance bends over her in an attitude of concern. I see her shake her head and wave him away coldly, dare I say viciously? As I sweep my eyes over the polished Sheraton table before me, I feel like a mortally wounded fighter on a ruined battlefield. Around me spilled wine, cigarette butts, mangled apples smudge the table's gleam.

Arthur folds his arm smoothly into Gwen's. His grasp, I see it at once, clamps itself onto her silken arm, and he bends to address her, nodding toward Elaine Becker. As I remember his concentration on Elaine all evening, my knees flutter again. Arthur's noble mien is not that of the confident seducer. Nor is he favoring Gwen with the derisive rictus of scorn. No, he wears an interested but professionally cool expression that I remember from a childhood pal of mine, a tough kid who enjoyed packing snowballs with rocks.

Too late, I understand this evening chez Sovern, should have realized that Arthur Sovern's decisive mind cloaks us all as completely as it covers the company. I should have known that he never relinquishes command. He has uncovered corporate disloyalty, and will move at once to eradicate it. And he never proceeds in any determination without consulting all available evidence. I failed him, failed to provide him with the information he needed. Acquiring it elsewhere, tonight he has assured himself of his correct analysis, and will soon issue directives for destruct. His marriage and Sovern PI will plunge into deepest, darkest recession. Still, being Arthur, he had no other choice.

I lean over the candles and try to blow them out, but my breath comes shallowly and the candles flicker. "I think the party's over," I whisper.

"On the contrary, Ezra," Arthur says over his shoulder, propelling Gwen like a wheelbarrow into the salon. "The party is only beginning. We would all be grateful for that renowned magic touch."

Gwen turns to give me a quizzical, fond glance. Fond, and final, I think. Even now, as Arthur's management skills detonate her willfulness, she has acquired the training to survive the fallout. She won't beg for forgiveness; she has gone beyond that, as I'm positive Arthur knows. She will not plead for another chance to show her loyalty to Sovern PI, as Lance will, knowing when she's lost her credibility. Gwen has outsmarted her mentors, donned a blast-proof suit, is prepared to face life after Sovern. But what about the rest of us, we lackeys who needed Gwen and Arthur, their favor and support? If I surmise correctly, Arthur, the complete manager, has decided to cut us all loose from Sovern's gravitational system. Lance will soon be cowering abjectly, for Arthur has probably already ordained Lance's setting sun. Flying home in fear and trembling, Lance will not even notice that the garage from hell has mutilated his beloved chariot. He will curse his fate and Elaine's emotional instability. The other guests will breathe sour relief at having avoided Apocalypse.

As for me, Ezra the Necromancer, I am revealed as a fraud who has fumbled his sleight of hand. I leave my refuge in the dining room for the unwelcome space of the Soverns' salon. Arlene Stone perches her size 18 on a Louis XV chair, balancing delicate porcelain and two Teuscher chocolates. I careen into her line of vision, brake, and dock. I grab one of her plump, soft hands. "Dear Mrs. Stone," I exhale carefully, "Our dinner conversation was so enlightening; I would consider it a great favor if you'd visit my workshop when you're next in town."

Goodbye, Friends

❁ ———————————— ❁

*S*now is a gauze curtain draped over Fifth Avenue. Under a No Parking, Violators Will Be Towed sign, Faith Weston coasts the old Volvo to a stop before the Metropolitan Museum of Art. Grateful at having escaped death on her treacherous drive from Larchmont, she emits little grunts of relief — "phew, uh, uh, uh, phew." For a brief minute she rests her head on the wheel, muttering, "You made it, kid." All the way down the Hutchinson River Parkway, navigating an early December snow storm, she has kept up her courage by talking to herself. Just like Dolores, she thinks. Talking to myself to assert that I'm still alive, going to make it. "All this white shit, and for another dumb party where I'm not needed or wanted. Nowhere else in the whole world would humans step outside their caves on nights like this."

She is intact — no multiple fractures or brain damage — after her slalom course along the Hutch, but an hour late. Since the dinner guests will spend the first hour oiling themselves into pliable table companions, she doesn't worry about her tardiness. She scuttles away from her car, assured that the dense snow will discourage tickets or towing. Later, she'll have to dig herself out, but for now, Faith is almost happy that across Fifth Avenue's cold landscape is her destination, a limestone oasis of noise and warmth that she had been previously dreading.

Earlier, when Tom had phoned with driving instructions to the Manhattan apartment, he had, with a journalist's clear eye and tart tongue, been objective about the evening. "It's true that Bill Hoyt doesn't know how to engage his brain before he puts his mouth in gear. He may be the country's most distinguished investment banker, but he can't wait to nail me for that takeout we did on him last week."

"Then why bother going to his boring parades of the rich and famous?" Faith had replied. "You don't enjoy any of those burning egos. And in this weather?"

"Because" — and here Faith heard the slight tinge of exasperation in Tom's voice, directed often at those who are ignorant of the way the world works — "the man has come down to our shop and talked to us many times, graciously. He's a good source. When he invites us to his parties to demonstrate our clout and his by association, it's only polite to go. You're obliged to reciprocate, Faith, in this rough-and-tumble world, respect the old quid pro quo."

"He's never said three words to me ever," Faith said. "I don't think he knows who I am. You're the one with the clout, as you call it, not me. The last time we were at one of the Hoyt shindigs, his wife asked me to pass the canapés."

Faith remembers the impatience tumbling across the telephone wires. "Don't be daft. Polly Hoyt has nothing to recommend her but big bucks. You know I hate going to these social things by myself. Didn't we marry for better or worse?"

Hanging up the phone, Faith thought yes, we did pledge that, but on examination of her bitten nails, she was not so sure. Ragged in the service of formidable anxiety, the nails seemed a metaphor for her life, something to be dealt with as she wished, for no one else really cared one way or the other. Her profession, creating advertising copy, could use polishing, too. Who needed lyrical odes to upscale plumbing fixtures? Faucets and valves, tub drains and shower rods were just that, functional objects necessary for the elimination of dirt and waste, whether they be solid brass, vitreous china, or the workhorse of the industry, cheap steel. Only her employer, O. J. Stein Advertising, and the client plumbing companies read or cared about the promises of "classic designs and color palettes for basins," or the "exciting array of spouts, handle styles, and finishes" she churned out to accompany four-color photographs of toilets and shower stalls. Once she had hoped for publishing or television.

And her marriage sometimes seemed as laughable as her profession. Was there enough there, enough that wasn't more than the predictable coupling of two middle-class, white, upwardly mobile adults? To keep the union intact, she had just put herself and the Volvo in jeopardy. Remembering the terrifying stem turns she had maneuvered around slow-moving salt-spreaders and stranded motorists, Faith shivers as the doorman directs her toward the proper elevator. She is damp and cold. The day has gone on too long. She should have spent her time buying a new dress. In uptown Manhattan, it is evident that her three-year-old dinner skirt and lace blouse lack style. Really, she could be a waitress late to work at a posh restaurant.

On the twelfth floor, the party is in full glow. Faith slides cautiously from the hand-painted elevator, hoping to blend somehow into 5,000 square feet aroar with the conversations of nuclear-powered self-esteem. She says her name — "Faith Weston" — to restore her larynx to working order, and accepts a glass of champagne from a smiling waiter. Before plunging into the crowd where Tom is hidden, she pauses for a moment under an eerie painting by someone named Enrico Baj. She recognizes a famous art critic for the magazine *Modern Identity* lecturing a TV producer and a feminist author, "Baj has lost the specificity of his former loaded references, and his new work has gained in resonance." The producer and author gaze solemnly at the painting, as if asking it for a satisfactory reply.

"Excuse me," Faith says, realizing too late that query, no matter how respectful, implies ignorance; that among these icons of power, it is fatal not to know both the questions *and* the answers. "What does that mean exactly?"

"What does what mean?" says the critic, pausing in his lecture and frowning at Faith as if he had caught her picking his pocket.

"What you just said, um, you know, about the specificity and the resonance. In layman's language."

"I don't write for laymen," the critic says.

"Sorry," says Faith. "Your expertise is so well known, I thought perhaps I'd be honored to receive some of it."

"I suggest you try my course at the New School, Beginning Art History."

The feminist looks a bit shocked at this rudeness, and she smiles sympathetically at Faith, but the TV producer jumps in. "Arthur, don't get distracted by beautiful women. You're making Baj totally accessible to me at last."

The critic turns his back on Faith and addresses the triptych's androids once more. A refrain pursues her: "A dialectic is ensuing here between the expansive, atmospheric haze above and the trapped, claustrophobic image below."

Faith grabs another champagne flute, and culls the crowd for her husband. Standing on tiptoe, unsteady in the roiling sea, she thinks that she is the only performer here without an audience, a supernumerary left in the wings. If only she could find Tom. He always runs interference. Perhaps she should look in the men's room.

Instead, she drags a smile across her teeth and inches over to the wall, pretending to escape the hubbub. The art critic is still at it. His pretentiousness reminds her of an earlier humiliation. She sees herself as she had been this morning, huddled on the back porch of her Larchmont house. A north wind predicting bad weather charged across Long Island Sound like an 18-wheeler, whistling under her down coat. Soon, it would snow.

She remembers the feel of the furnace pumping thermal bliss under her feet. Through the walls she caught the wails of the vacuum cleaner and of Dolores, the Colombian housekeeper, as she attacked the dust and a Spanish song from her childhood: "*Adios, muchachos, compañeros, de mi vida.*"

At first, the cold of the porch hadn't seemed so desperate. The old furnace was faulty, and Faith often took a walk to clear her sinuses of the scent of oil. She was exhilarated to be outside with snow about to fall, alone with memories of her childhood in Binghamton, winters of icy delight.

But catching Dolores's song reminded her of the foolish plans she had once had for the two of them, one from a foreign country, thousands of air miles and a different language away, the other a transplant from upstate New York, two once-simple *muchachas* coping with dislocation and loneliness, who together would defy suburbia. When Dolores first sang those mournful songs about her youthful sunny days and languorous nights, Faith had felt a kinship, although she had never been south of Charleston. When Dolores sang longingly of the friends of her childhood, fiesta-loving *compañeros* she would never see again, unless economic and political conditions improved, Faith empathized with the agony of losing your old pals. Even though they both had husbands and jobs, and Dolores five small children at home in New Rochelle with her unemployed spouse, nonetheless Faith had improbably expected girlish confidences. After a few weeks of wild abandonment performing sisterly, house-cleaning salsas together, Faith imagined herself and Dolores becoming dear friends.

She stamped her feet on the cold deck, angry that sisterhood with her housekeeper, like many another of her dreams, had gone unrealized.

Was it my fault, she wondered, that my exhausting job, and Tom's, plus the after-hours socializing, didn't leave me time to develop a friendship? And Dolores had been so efficient, for the first five years a mystery machine who arrived every morning after her employers caught the 7:06 New Haven Railroad to New York City, and left before they returned exhausted at 8 P.M. or later. For five days a week and $300, Dolores whipped the house into shape, shopped, dealt with UPS and bossed the gardener, the garbageman, and any other souls who ventured onto her turf at 85 Byron Lane. Every night, some variation of a Spanish dish rested warmly in the oven to greet the returning commuters. Faith became accustomed to the luxury. Only sometimes, she wondered what happened when Dolores returned to her own large family. When did she cook for them or clean or take some time for herself? Faith vowed that one day, when she had more time, she would find out more of Dolores's private affairs.

But she hadn't, and there she was, on a freezing back porch amid wet firewood and discarded magazines, not behaving like an adult, more like an abused animal, whining pitifully with her tail between her legs. Pathetic it was — like the little match girl in the fairy tale.

Another waiter approaches. Faith grabs a third drink, mindful of the consequences. Tom is lost, perhaps forever. Then, she sees next to her a woman reporter from Tom's magazine, who Tom says has brass balls. She is talking to a former secretary of labor who was once Faith's tennis partner at a charity benefit. Had they won? "Hello," Faith says to the couple, "is this a private conversation or can I play, too?"

The secretary glances at her. "Faith, you cute thing. How's the backhand?" Without waiting for an answer, he says to the reporter, "Want to go to Syria with me next week? We'll get some good interviews; Assad and I are buddies."

The reporter gives Faith a vague smile, and pulls a tiny date book from her evening purse. "I can't go until Wednesday. But seriously, Seth, could we hit Arafat, too? A month ago, he promised me an hour and then he blew me off to go to Libya."

Secretary Seth gazes at the ceiling. The reporter puts her head close to his and whispers. He laughs. "Water skiing in the Gulf after," he promises. They are continents away from Faith and the wintry scene beyond the window.

❊ ——————— ❊

Lost in thoughts of missed opportunities, Faith began to feel the penetrating cold of the December northeaster. Dolores had proved to be a perfect housekeeper, a good cook, and so reliable that neither her children's illnesses nor her own occasional aches prevented her from showing up in Larchmont like a faithful, Spanish cyborg. After five years Faith almost forgot what she looked like, and their fractured English conversations by phone became more infrequent.

But now it had been six months since Faith had decided writing ad copy in a gray tower in Manhattan, two train rides away, was getting old, that she could easily retire from deli heartburn and overtures from a boss in midlife crisis to freelance in her attic office, prepare for motherhood. Tom approved. He was working long hours, falling like a stone into bed each night. "Why should both of us endure the commute from hell? Why not stay home? Now that I'm managing editor, I see the beginning of good things for us, and this old boy wants kids. We're not getting any younger."

Faith immediately wrote copy in her mind, paragraphs about gracious living. She and Dolores together in the old house, Dolores dispensing hourly cups of Red Zinger and maternal advice, she writing brilliantly, at the same time producing perfect children in domestic harmony and Spanglish bliss. But Dolores had plans of her own.

Here are the results of my plans, Faith thought, looking around her, at the porch, a deck really, constructed by the former owners, a cheap addition to the old Victorian, and open to the elements. She had never really noticed it before. She crouched on an untidy mound of firewood, staring at a garden which, in December, was a bleak ruin watched over by the giant eye of her neighbor's satellite dish on the other side of the fence. Beam me up, too, she thought, up and away, to rocketing space vehicles, away from the cold and my misery.

At first, when Faith became homebound, Dolores had just been uncooperative, seemingly too busy for buddying. She cleaned, washed, and ironed in ruminating solitude. Faith decided to give her housekeeper time to adjust. For five years, her employer safely out of the way, Dolores had fantasized at will, by day happily free of roaches, needy children, jobless husband. The old Victorian on Byron Lane, a crazy mix of turrets and gables that only Stephen King would envy, was Dolores's castle, her refuge from reality. In gratitude, five days a week she endowed her dream house with massive potions of Chlorox and mildew remover, scoured it to the bleach of bones. She showed no interest in seeking another position, a larger wage, a more compatible employer. Faith had often searched for clues to the mystery of Dolores: a soiled apron, a balled handkerchief, a lingering scent of labor-intensive body odor. In vain. Dolores left each day having scrubbed away her identity with the dirt from the kitchen counters.

The situation worsened. Dolores refused Faith's offers to join her over a Campbell's soup lunch. Perhaps she hated canned soup. More likely, Dolores found conversation too difficult. Ignorance of each other's language had been no hindrance when one was safely out of the way all day. Faith suffered the ache of monolingual despair.

Gradually, she felt cast as the wicked witch in Dolores's fairy tale, a menace to be repelled at all costs. Each day, the bustle below became more intense, confining Faith to her office, unable to concentrate on her ad copy. While working her way through yet another crossword puzzle, she strained to hear word from below. Dolores worked in delighted bliss, answered the phone and hailed the mailman in acceptable broken English, all the while ignoring Faith, the prisoner in her tower. Sometimes Faith would descend the stairs tentatively, determined to seize the initiative. Too often, she rushed back to the attic, fearful of noisy confrontation. Sadly, she concluded that Dolores would never relinquish her oasis. *She* would have to surrender. It was only a matter of weeks before the last bastion, the office where Faith fretted and worked out eight-letter words for stress, fell to the enemy.

And so no dinner parties emerged from the old house on Byron Lane, little lively copy from the attic, no pregnancy. Faith complained to Tom of Dolores's fascistic hand. He said, "My mother always said two women in the same house could never get along. Why don't you get out, see friends, do some shopping? You need new clothes." His words were implicit reproof of her management skills.

From her prickly perch on the firewood, Faith strained to hear if Dolores had finished abusing the attic office, permitting a return to the house's warmth. Stein had said he needed the copy on portrait Victorian bathtubs by tomorrow. She should be upstairs, booting up her IBM. But the whine of the vacuum and the boisterous songs quelled her. She stayed where she was, fear and cold damping down a last spark of courage.

Storm-tossed and drifting, Faith comes upon Tom in a corner of the Hoyt apartment where, true to his earlier prediction, their host is confronting him. Tom chews smoked salmon, his face solemn.

"I don't want you to think I'm complaining, Tom, but that piece you people did on me. Your reporter is completely ignorant about Third World economic management. For starters, he had Nigeria confused with Tanzania, and as for liberalized marketing and pricing, we dialogue, not dictate . . ." Faith watches Tom redden.

She concentrates as diligently as three glasses of choice champagne will permit, restraining the impulse to cover Tom with kisses, drag him to the floor. She shakes hands carefully with the host, thanks him for the invitation. She is aware she has interrupted the men's game at a crucial moment, that neither her husband nor Hoyt seem eager to have the subject changed. But she can't help herself. She says, "Mr. Hoyt, perhaps it's more advantageous for your blood pressure not to read villainous accounts of yourself. Try reading the ads, instead. They really mellow you out."

There is a loud silence. Tom and the financier look embarrassed for each other.

Earlier, snow began to fall on Larchmont, vague flakes like ash spitting from the Sound, before Faith realized she was still huddled on the fire logs, sniffling and riffling through a soggy *New Yorker.* The magazine's December issues often featured her plumbing copy accompanied by fine-grain, artsy photos of toilets and basins. The thermometer by the kitchen door registered 32 degrees. What craziness was this, Faith asked herself, not finding a Stein ad anywhere. How could I have sunk to this rotten-apple bottom, out here in the snow, while inside Dolores sings in oil-heated bliss? It was freezing, literally, and even though she should have left her office while Dolores cleaned it, fleeing the house was an admission of total defeat. If she caught pneumonia, and had to be hospitalized, she would probably never again be admitted through the red front door of 85 Byron Lane.

When earlier she had heard Dolores's shout up to her office, *"Vámanos, mujer!"* and watched her storm up the attic stairs like a gladiator with Hoover and trash-bag weaponry, the Spanish equivalent of "Let's go, woman!" her battlecry, Faith had wished for the hundredth time she could bolt the door against the attack, before she was swept along with the dust and innocent paper clips.

But there was no door to the attic, and even if there had been, Faith thought sadly, I would still allow myself to be intimidated. What had happened to my youthful determination, the stubborn persistence that had propelled me out of Binghamton? Nothing could stop her, hadn't she worked her way through Syracuse sorting and packing apples? Hadn't she found a job with O. J. Stein almost immediately after arriving in the city? The pay had seemed incredible, and then she met Tom. She had been in ecstasy, grateful for her luck.

Faith tried an experimental moan, a low, inhuman growl. This untenable position on the porch was the final humiliation, the last vestige of a shrinking will. Dolores had become her newest boss, exercising a different kind of harassment, criticizing her schedule, her eating habits, her being there. When she heard the sound of her housekeeper's key in the lock each morning, she murmured in pain. Dolores had turned her into an unwanted animal, lurking about the house, scratching at windows. She grabbed an umbrella leaning against the kitchen door, and sat down again on the chopped wood, the umbrella raised against the snow and the television dish, her arms hugging her cold legs. Was it too late to learn mastery over her fate, halt this headlong flight from reality? Could she stop biting her nails? She stared down at the hated extremities. They were blue with cold, and ugly, where once they had been manicured and colored Hot Red every Thursday.

Faith felt a trickle of tear slide down her cheek, her body sag in defeat. She was being vacuumed into oblivion. She opened the *New Yorker* again. And a miracle happened.

The magazine, soggy but intact, fell open to an advertisement for the Chubb Group of insurance companies. In four colors, a handsome couple reclined on burnt-orange club chairs in a library, wood-paneled and lined with books and Chinese art objects. The couple wore evening clothes, but he had removed his tux jacket and she, in a white satin dinner dress with a slit to the knee, had kicked off her golden slippers. His dark hair receding a bit. She — slim, blonde, with carved cheekbones — drinking from a fragile demitasse. He from a wine glass. Two crystal decanters sparkling on the antique table between them. A graceful grand piano, from which a gigantic bouquet of roses, tulips and apple blossoms sprang. Luminous studio lighting.

Faith studied the photograph carefully, forgetting for a moment her chill, dropping the umbrella, wiping away the snow flakes. Here was the life she craved. She gave the two models names and pronounced them through numbed lips. "Alexandra, Elliot, you do have a lovely life."

Alexandra and Elliott would freak at her ridiculous

state of banishment, freezing on an open porch in December while the bangs of the Hoover against the office baseboards reverberated overhead. They wouldn't have fled to the Safeway or to another shopping expedition. Calmly, they would address Dolores in her native tongue, instructing her on her duties, which she would perform willingly, happily, at the same time helping them arrange the flowers, pour the drinks.

Faith smiled at the Chubb ad. Like struck matches, it warmed her, informed her about pride and strength, spoke of authority that could be learned, that was more than a trace element found only in the hardest rocks. The photograph shouted at her to do something. Take charge, it said. Remember those childhood friends in Binghamton, angry rebels who marched out to fight for a brave new world of love not war, eager to total the military-industrial complex. They had been the real players, impatient at me for burying myself in the stacks of Central Binghamton High's library, far away from picketing Dow Chemical.

Snow flakes falling painlessly on her face, Faith stood up and like a conductor before an orchestra, began to whirl her arms in triumph. She was suddenly warm, her movements strong and brave, her thoughts propelling her limbs. She *could* make her world, the one whose possibilities were once as ripe as the Cortlands in her father's orchard, delicious. And for Dolores, too, we can work on her dreams. When she left her Cartagena hovel, her friends envying her for heading for New Rochelle, the far side of Paradise, it wasn't her fault that she had found fewer sweets here than in her sixteenth-birthday *piñata*.

Alexandra and Elliot are saying it's never too late to stop being a dreamer, we can change water into wine, teach the clumsy to tango, restore power outages. Faith saw Tom and herself later in the evening, returning from their fourth business outing in two weeks, stepping into the Chubb ad, suffering neither their usual headaches nor fatigue. Tom would gently remove her satin dress as they sank gracefully onto the worn oriental rug that had belonged to his grand- mother. Offstage, Dolores would be heard murmuring dis- creetly, "*Los niños, los niños.*" The next day, Faith would begin to direct her destiny with a passable imitation of Alexandra's easy, sure grace.

Soaked with snow, the models' aristocratic faces began to fade from the magazine page. I must be finally hallucinat- ing, Faith thought, as she heard from inside Dolores's bellow. "*Qué pasa ahora?*" Faith groaned and extended her icy legs, aware she was cracking irrevocably, a Humpty-Dumpty of the suburbs.

"What's happening now?" erupted regularly like a con- quistador's war cry from her housekeeper's lips. What was it, what inert, innocent thing — a hamper of soiled clothes, spilled kitty litter, drooping gladiolas — that was provoking today's ire?

Faith directed her protesting body toward the kitchen door, rehearsing supplicating words. She would comfort Dolores, assure her that she was loved, wanted, had nothing to fear. A blast of arctic air rushed in with her, prompting a yell from somewhere nearby, "Shit, *qué pasa ahora?*"

Faith paused by the sink, massaged her cold fingers, rearranged her frozen lips. There was a bang, and Dolores burst through the swinging doors of the kitchen. Faith looked at her hopefully, noting the motherly bulk, the capa- ble hands, the sturdy back.

"*Ponga la mesa, lave los platos, barra los cuartos, sacuda los muebles."* Dolores muttered to herself. Without a word, she swept by Faith to empty the dust bag into the garbage pail. Me, too, Faith thought, I'm as disposable as the litter, as inanimate as the table, the dishes, the furniture Dolores attacks so strenuously. She wants me out of her way so she can do what is necessary to survive.

Faith leaned on the sink, her boots dripping dirty snow onto the kitchen floor. Dolores noticed, too. The two women glared at each other, and Faith said, "I think I'll do some grocery shopping. *Qué necessita?"* Dolores began to scrub up the wet, while Faith suited up for the Safeway.

Oh, Alexandra and Elliot, you can't change the world. The best I can produce is garbage about gold-plated faucets and matching soap dishes. And my old friends, those models for future generations, the rebels who were going to change the world, where are they now? Still in Binghamton, selling Toyotas and real estate, still fighting, it's true, but today it's to pay the mortgage and keep the kids in school. And envying me, my life of ease. They're as out of it as Dolores's friends, imaginations warped by time and experience.

Tonight, Tom and I will drive home from the party in humor as foul as the weather. The Volvo will cough its protest along the Hutch, while Tom, still annoyed by his host's accusations, will remind me again about that green slime seeping into the basement despite the plumber's assurances and megabills. I will have a sour stomach from anxiety and too much wine. And I will only ever, ever escape from Dolores by burying myself in aisles of Lestoil and Lysol tub cleaner.

In a gesture of rage, Faith ripped the Chubb ad from the magazine, stepped around Dolores to stuff the page into the garbage grinder. Flipped the switch that sent Alexandra and Elliot into a biodegradable afterlife.

❀ ───────── ❀

The snow is a wall outside the Hoyts' apartment window, the world hidden in white smoke and dreams. Perhaps we will all have to spend the night, Faith thinks. She wanders away from Tom and the host. She locates the waiter with the champagne, and slips herself and the glass through an open door next to the fireplace. A wave of recognition strikes her. The library she has stepped into might have served as a model for that Chubb ad she was admiring early in the day, the gracious home of Alexandra and Elliot's imaginary lives. The same warm, walnut patina, the smell of leather-bound books and furniture polish trickling from odd corners. The volumes worn and old. Some are signed on the title page with the spidery signature of the host's great-grandma, a lady of learning among nineteenth-century robber barons. One day, Faith thinks, I intend to have a library like this. Only classics and first editions, in a climate that asks for nothing but curiosity, where no one, not Dolores or art critics or even husbands dare enter.

She selects *My Ántonia* from its bed between Capote and Cervantes. She settles down in a comfortable leather arm-chair, and begins to read. From page 15, she reads aloud, "The red of the grass made all the great prairie the colour of wine-stains, or of certain seaweeds when they are first washed up."

Absorbed in the lost lady's story, Faith does not hear someone enter the library.

Ablaze in diamonds, Polly Hoyt shimmers like Cather's prairie. "Faith, my dear, what are you doing in here alone? You must come out; the Ambassador is eager to dine . . ."

Faith clings to her distraction like a lifeboat.

"Oh, Mrs. Hoyt," she says, "I was reading Willa Cather. Don't you just love her? Listen to this great passage."

The hostess sighs, sets a smile over her large teeth. "Dear, I'm sure I'd love to, but dinner must begin. Do come along now." She disappears in a perfumed rush.

Faith's little island has metamorphosed into an atomic atoll. She considers locking herself in the powder room. But Tom will only bang on the door. "Faith, what's the matter? Polly Hoyt said you were looking a bit under the weather. Come on, everyone has gone in to dinner." His voice will have that note of anxiety that appears when he misplaces things — his datebook, his socks, her.

Faith slowly closes *My Ántonia,* and drains the champagne glass. She stuffs the story of sturdy pioneer women coping with disease, bigotry, death under the fat cushion of the club chair. She takes off her shoes, black satin pumps that pinch her toes, and lines them up neatly between the chair legs. She unbuttons her blouse and hangs it on the chair's back. She unzips her dinner skirt. It slides to the floor in a black puddle, leaving her in a white satin slip, frayed at the hem and tight around her middle. Here she is, a little dizzy and fuzzy, but nonetheless in satin, authentically Alexandra at last.

December, late evening. Blizzard in progress. Faith addresses her stockinged feet. "*Adios, muchachos,*" and then, "*Vámanos, mujer,*" she says, and glides only a little unsteadily to join Elliot in the dining room.

Cheating Despair

*A*round the middle of March, quite suddenly, I died.

This occurrence created only a minor ripple in our ocean of public events. The *Chatham Crier* did an adequate obit: "Popular 45-year-old motel owner dies suddenly. Former president of the JayCees." You know the sort of thing. They ran a picture of me from when I had more hair.

Frank Bellows, the editor of the *Crier,* who had once tried to blackball my application to the golf club, said to his publisher, "How is it that no cause of death was listed? A 45-year-old bachelor dies mysteriously? Sounds like AIDS to me."

A typical comment from a fevered imagination. It's tough to be single in a small town where colossally ignorant people like Bellows speculate about your private life. When the *Crier* published a piece under his byline about pervasive corruption in our county, he played up Marty's massage parlor. Before Marty closed for good, she told me Bellows included her in the article because she decided to start charging him.

Other, kinder folks said it was a shame about my Mama, who worked so hard to help me, and only wanted a couple of grandbabies for her trouble.

Five days a week Mama shared the front office with a five-inch TV, working at reception while I busied myself with handyman chores and Jeannette swept and wiped her way through the dozen rooms. At least once a week, after attending to the elegant men on "The Guiding Light" and "All My Children," Mama bustled down the aisles of Jackson's Department Store, seeking in vain for her son the double-vented suits and narrow ties that spelled video success.

She's a world-class shopper, anyway, and the day after my funeral, Mama gathered up all the boxes from my closet. She threw down on the counter at Jackson's two ties, an opened package of undershorts and a two-year-old shirt, and told the scandalized clerk, "My son had a charge account here for years. Of course, you'll take back these things he never wore."

At the grave site, she cried copiously, between the ugly hacks of emphysema. "So young, so much to live for. To think he went before me." For 25 years, I sprayed Lysol Disinfectant in vain against the fumes of Mama's Camel Filters. But I never complained, and she rewarded me with a sincere display of her sorrow.

Others at the service kept their counsel. They knew, or thought they did, my real secrets.

My friend Billy held the urn where reposed my mortal remains and then placed it carefully on the flip side of the stone that said Collins. In a shallow hole, I rested comfortably next to my sister Coriander, dead at age four. Meredith, my lover of record, laid a stiff bouquet of gladiolas over the hole and recited dramatically, "Between the desire and the spasm / Between the potency and the existence / Between the essence and the descent / Falls the shadow."

Billy used to visit me on January evenings, braving icy roads to have a breather from Rochelle and the kids. We turned off the Vacancy sign, and I pretended I was in Florida, where the motel business flourished 12 months of the year. The TV flickered and the logs in the fireplace crackled like cellophane.

"Cozy," Billy would say, cuddling a Miller Lite. "You're cool, man, no strings. Your own boss, good help — your ma and Jeannette. Let's face it, marriage stinks. Rochelle said she had all those kids cause she was tired of menstruating."

Billy, as usual, was only half right. I was glad not to have Rochelle, who smelled like unaired sheets, and those bilious kids. But running a rural motel with only a mother and a slow-witted cleaning girl for company sometimes seemed sad.

Meredith and I had a good thing going for a while. A divorced city chick looking for different strokes, she was fun in spurts. She never told anyone I sometimes let rooms to local teenagers for weekend quickies. And she kept out of Mama's way.

But then she started accusing me. "Your soul is so untidy," she said, "good grooming can't disguise that." Perhaps she was referring to the way Ken McKnight, the doctor's 18-year-old, sneaked regularly into the motel with the wife of Jim Bellows, the newspaper editor. "Why are you so scared to lay your emotional cards on the table?" That was Meredith in postcoital pique.

Joke: She was good as women go, and as women go, she went. Then I watched in envy when Ken McKnight came in asking for room 12, the farthest from the office. I saw Alice Bellows move like a shadow from the car into the room.

Jeannette came by just then, the Hoover cord slung over her arm. She saw me staring out the window. "Mister Geordie, don't be sad. They're together." She touched my shoulder. "Number 12's a real nice room. It's sunny and next to the garden."

It *was* a nice room and I spent my last hour there. I wasn't sad at all. Jeannette was smiling up at me, her skinny arms as dexterous with my body as with the bathroom floors. The gray sheets smoothed over us like a queen's satin. For once, I wasn't checking out the plumbing or worrying about a loan to replace the carpets. Tongues of sunlight licking my bare shoulders hinted of languorous, tropical climes. I decided Jeannette deserved a trip to Florida.

"Mister Geordie, don't work so hard," I heard Jeannette say. I remember making little noises, possibly of gratitude.

Are We Almost There?

❈ ———————————— ❈

*O*nce upon a time, when they were about one-tenth of the way south on the Jersey Turnpike, Ginger cried out, "There's bananas in this car and I'm gonna puke." Once upon a time, Chris held his mother's hand outside Bergdorf's window and boasted, "Someday I'm gonna buy you that fuzzy coat up there." Now, Ginger has a punky hairdo and runs a male burlesque in Patchogue. Chris and the lynx coat are gone.

K., gravity pulling her chin and stomach beyond hope or surgery, cultivates her garden. She also specializes in rescuing drowning creatures from the swimming pool. Sometimes it is too late: the filter system serves up bloated frogs, headless sparrows, limp rabbits. K. mourns. She prefers death to take place in secret, in the woods, behind hospital doors. Not in a tangle of metal and limbs on the highway or in the trap of her filter system. She prefers doctors who say, "You do not now have a fatal illness nor will you ever."

Ginger, on the other hand, approaches illness with relish and neurosis with enthusiasm. Catastrophe and phobias are her food and drink. She is now lounging around her mother's pool, nude except for three cartridge belts wrapped around her tiny waist.

K. fishes into her pool and rescues a yellow jacket whirling into oblivion on a sycamore leaf. She avoids looking at her daughter's brown body, glistening with coconut oil. She prays that the neighbor's housekeeper won't appear across the lawn, tendering some zucchini from her garden. Ginger is at ease, the cartridges tattooing her tender skin, talking idly about her friends.

"It's demeaning to have to ask your husband for every cent you need. Yves gives Sally money for her yoga and her music lessons and her makeup. Is he a father figure or what?"

K. deposits the dizzy wasp on the ground and begins to snip the dead heads off the coreopsis. Experience cautions her against replying spontaneously to her daughter's analysis.

She turns over a leaf to look for slugs. Bananas trap them, she's been told. Banana peels strewn around the garden decimate pests. Take your bananas into the garden, also your eggshells and coffee grounds, not on car trips. But she is calculating a reply just the same.

"Perhaps Sally's an old-fashioned girl." Surely that's innocuous enough, perhaps even an affirmation of Ginger's own thoughts. No.

Ginger snaps, her attention turned away from the coconut oil basting, "And Yves's a sacrificial neurotic. A martyr to love. Like Chris calling you Our Lady of the Sorrows."

Bang! Ginger has fired one of her cartridges into K.'s vital organs. K. gets off her knees, puts the clippers neatly back into the basket along with the spent coreopsis, and heads for the shed and the spray gun. The roses have black-spot fungus.

K. likes the smell of the shed, a mixture of mildew and fertilizer. No one else ever enters. Her tears fall onto the Phygon XL, a chemical deadly to fungus and, perhaps, humans. She sits down on a nail barrel, across from a row of dried hydrangeas and baby's breath molting in their spiderweb hats.

When Ginger was a wiry, buck-toothed kid, she talked her younger brother into diving off a six-foot wall to test some nylon wings she'd fashioned. Later, when Chris was strung with wires and pulleys in his hospital bed, Ginger argued with the doctor about impact force versus the human body. Her present unusual career is the result of a Wharton School thesis on "Most Profitable Service Occupations in the 90s."

K. wipes her eyes with her blouse, because in a moment Ginger, regretting her rashness, will come looking for her mother, to apologize. Sure enough, here she is at the shed door, hair spiked like exclamation points from her oily skull, with a towel wrapped around the cartridges. She peers into the gloom. "Sorry, Ma, I'm a bitch." She spies something in the corner. "Hey, it's the kite. Pass it out, okay?"

K. lifts the kite from the shelf, blows off the dust and hands it to Ginger. They examine it in silence. A Japanese war kite, a huge eye with spidery eyelashes on a cerulean background, its sequined tail in shreds.

How they sweated four summers ago to get that kite to fly. Stumbling through the warm sand, they tripped, fell, laughed as the kite dipped and swayed, then crashed into the sea. Patiently, they manipulated it once again into the scoured sky. Then, Chris and Ginger screamed in unison as the contraption, its Liza Minelli eye sparkling, soared, tamed by their teamwork on the double strings. For a time, the sticks and paper held them all in a haze of happiness.

"It's had it, Ma," Ginger says, fingering the ripped sequins. "Let's toss it and buy a new one." She goes behind the shed, and K. hears the garbage lid open. Crack. Rip. Ginger forces the cross members into the can. K. looks at her fungicide.

"I'll get lunch while you do the roses," Ginger says, and takes her nakedness away from the neighbors' eyes.

K. is of two minds about the roses. They're a holdover from the previous owners of the property, two oldsters who fussed over and pampered the hybrid teas and floribundas like ambitious parents, rewarded by spectacular blooms that won prizes. Ginger and her father think the rose garden takes too much of K.'s effort. They propose a tennis court.

K., who daily dispatches Japanese beetles to their deaths in cups of turpentine, sprays weekly for mildew and aphids, and wills the roses to survive in spite of their traumas, wonders herself if these Olympians of nature's art warrant such nurturing. But the scent of ripening roses always gives her second thoughts.

"Beauty is its own excuse for being," she murmurs, then looks around guiltily. Literary clichés are but one of K.'s indulgences.

Even without the roses, the garden's beauty is a strain on the skills of one woman and an unreliable local boy. It has the look of disorder on the march — presumptuous weeds, tumbled peonies, Virginia creeper stalking and strangling.

But K. finds the confusion reassuring, nature's own competition. She prefers this to burying the rose garden under an Omni tennis court.

André Watts playing Gershwin drifts into the garden. The lush, sentimental melodies harmonize with the cicadas' whir. Ginger uses Gershwin as music to strip by, and often choreographs movements in K.'s living room. What's happened to lunch?

The sun has K. dizzy. She heads for the terrace. The grape vines are heavy with this year's crop of Concords. She's glad she insisted on the pruning. The herb garden drowses next to the kitchen door.

K. experiences:

A pastiche of grapes, basil, sun.

A crazy quilt of tension, fatigue, helplessness.

An illusion of X-ray emissions, cosmic ray bursts.

She sinks under the global shade of the terrace umbrella, reminding herself to wear a sun hat next time out.

And gardening gloves, too. Ugly hands, unmanicured. Veins bulging like blue rivers at the flood. And brown spots, of course, which neither Porcelana nor Esotérica will bleach away. Dirty, grubby garden hands, once they played Gershwin, too. K. drops the offending members into her lap.

Ginger is not choreographing. She slides open the kitchen screen and appears with a tray bearing shrimp salad, bagel crisps, iced tea — a contrite lover with a peace offering. K. loves her desperately.

Ginger's cartridges now decorate an apron, embossed with a recipe for Alice B. Toklas cookies and a flash line, "Marijuana doesn't rot your teeth." The apron links Ginger to conventional domesticity. K. approves.

Then Ginger turns back for the utensils and K. breaks into a laugh. Ginger's buttocks, hard and brown from sunlamps and Nautilus workouts, are bare. The apron is merely a buffer between coconut oil and shrimp salad.

"I like your outfit."

"My guys use this getup for one of their numbers. 'Three Little Maids.' The iced tea is too sweet. Why do you buy this packaged junk?"

"Maybe I'm too lazy to make it from scratch. Um, what kind of men are your guys, anyway?" K. is not really curious. She has never set foot in Ginger's establishment. Most of her friends have, though, out of curiosity, pity. They report in stunning detail, seeming to accuse K. of aiding and abetting misconduct. "I mean, where do they come from?"

"They're not freaks if that's what you mean." Ginger laughs. "They need the money, but they don't have hang-ups about the work. One's even in law school. It's a job. It pays well. Far from this world, sure, but what isn't?"

Ginger spreads her arms wide to encompass the *House Beautiful* scene, one that, in fact, several shelter magazines have photographed. The linden tree undulates over the turquoise pool, and the grass rolls down to the pond, a runway to center stage. A family of swans swims into stage right.

"Rhapsody in Blue" floats out the window under Watts's fluid fingers, and K. tries to imagine getting down to the G-string (jock strap?) to the sounds of America's musical icon. Will Bach be next?

"Come in, Ma, come in." Ginger is staring at her mother across the table, wigwagging. "I said, do you think Dad will spring for the twenty thou?"

K. stalls. "Well, just last year he gave you the ten for redecorating."

Ginger is impatient with temporizing. She gets up, turns her back on K., sticks a foot in the pool, rescues a linden blossom. She tucks it behind her ear, an aproned mermaid in a chlorine sea.

"I paid it back. Now this opportunity won't wait."

"Opportunity?"

"Stop spacing, Ma. In Atlantic City."

The linden blossoms waft their perfume to the table as they drift into the pool. K. thinks sadly they'll end up in the filter system with the other detritus. She tries to concentrate.

"A new strip joint in Atlantic City?"

"A pleasure palace, please! Along with the gambling. The old ladies go for the young bods."

K. feels the shrimp salad rising on a wave of disgust. She sucks hastily at the iced tea, her diaphragm contracts, and she burps. "Oh, Ginger, there's more to life than the bottom line. Atlantic City's full of awful people — gamblers, drug dealers, Mafia."

Ginger rolls her eyeballs. "Horse shit. You're such a snob — the world according to the Junior League."

"Wait, wait . . . you don't have to use that language."

Ginger pounces as if lying in wait. "Who do you think keeps the local real estate firms booming around here? Who do you think your neighbors are?"

"Who?"

"Crooks, felons, living on big estates with swimming pools and art collections. They just leave their sleazy customers outside."

What on earth does Ginger mean? K. knows that her corner of paradise is not peopled by candidates for the vice squad. But she sees the disaster-bound train hurtling down the track. "You know that's not true," she insists. "You know our friends, you went to school with their children."

Ginger winds up. "Listen, for your information, I'm going to make B-school history. Do you know, I'm only one of four from my class to go into business for myself? *Self* Magazine is thinking of doing a cover story on me. Jesus, why are you jealous of what you can't control?"

K. pushes away from the table. A yellow jacket is helping itself to her unfinished salad anyway.

Ginger, her face sulky, steps out of the pool, snatches up the remains of lunch and disappears into the house.

Inside, Chick Corea's piano replaces Gershwin, quirky, themeless. K. hears Ginger speaking briskly, hooked up to her life-support system, the telephone. She sounds like a boss.

"No, Dante, that's not enough." Is Dante the costume designer, ready to add more material to the G-strings to placate the League of Decency? It seems he's an accountant.

Thunder murmurs in the distance. Ginger's voice rises. "Dante, the earnings ratio has got to rise before we can say our merchandising effort is successful. Maybe the product presentation could stand improvement."

K. has a vision of Ginger's product, the "bod," enticing as a Belgian chocolate. Clouds appear in the east. The pond turns greasy gray. A summer shower is approaching. As if they feel invisible under the clouds, three bunnies streak across the lawn, heading for lunch in K.'s garden.

Yes, I am jealous, what an awful thing to admit. K. remembers Ginger at 12, gritting her teeth and stripping gears round and round the driveway, determined to learn to drive. Since then, an alien in life-style, hairdo, clothes.

Thousands on psychotherapy to shed penis envy and promote effective ego management.

More telephone hookups. To Hal, the current lover, to a couple of bods. Will she call her father? She does, frequently, a dutiful daughter. But Jack is away. Ginger hangs up the phone. The toilet flushes, and she reappears, nods graciously to her mother. "How about a swim?"

Without waiting for an answer, she dives into the pool and methodically crawls her way up and down, up and down, as if her strokes could carry her into a nirvana of the slim and ambitious. K. wraps her arms around her legs and counts the laps — 21, 22, 23. Again, a love welling in her throat, or is it the shrimp salad of envy?

She's doing something with her life, something I don't much like, but she's got it in the grip of her beautiful straight white teeth. Chris and I, we flashed our molars and expected the world to smile back.

Two things happen. Somewhere (in memory? in Chick Corea's recorded-in-front-of-a-live-audience?) a tinkle of laughter floats out to the pool.

Ginger lifts her head, K. too. Almost immediately, a growl of thunder, closer and insistent, cancels the laugh. Ginger swims double-time to the end of the pool, climbs out and wraps herself in a dry towel. "Going to storm," she says. "Let's batten down." In a flurry of activity, she furls the umbrella, secures the chairs, whisks off the table the salt and pepper and the little vase of daisies. "The weatherman didn't say a word about thunderstorms today."

"Good for the flowers," K. says automatically. Ginger is as terrified of storms as she is of airplanes. But K. knows her domain is secure, nothing can disturb the serenity, certainly not a summer storm. She doesn't want to go into the chilly, slightly dank, house.

"Remember when you were kids?" K. says, peering through the kitchen door at Ginger just inside, surveying the sky and dripping water over the Mexican tiles. "How you'd all pile on my bed when it stormed? Remember how Jem would bark and try to pull you off me?"

Ginger says, "I remember how Jem used to pull me off the bed. He'd never touch Chris."

"You teased the poor dog unforgivably." But K. sees Ginger in a heap on the floor, crying to get back on the bed, the big, white Lab pulling her pajamas, growling over her, while Chris lay curled up among the pillows, placid and quiet.

Ginger whines, a comic imitation of childhood. "You didn't even notice."

K. slides inside the door, takes her daughter's arm. Ginger's hand, without freckle or vein, is long-fingered, capable, smooth. Her nails are bitten.

"Notice? You were born to be noticed. And I notice now that you're dripping on my floor."

Ginger snatches her hand from her mother's and darts into the little bath to dry off.

K. wanders into the living room. The rumble of thunder is coming closer, heavy artillery across no-man's-land. The old 12-paned windows are beginning to shake and rattle. The swans on the pond, distracted, their feathers ruffling, bustle around looking for the lee. The house is dense with humidity, sticky, airless.

Ginger reappears, dressed in a dry towel, turns up the stereo, closes the windows, paces. "Wait for the windows until it starts to rain," pleads K. Ginger takes no notice. Like a scout alert for the enemy, she prowls around the airless room, touching a book, fondling a chocolate, turning off the stereo.

K. sits placidly amid the cabbage roses of the sofa cover. She hums a tuneless melody to keep from thinking of a recurrent nightmare. She, Ginger and Chris have turned over their sailboat in just such a storm. Half-dead with fear and exhaustion, they are cast up on a hummock of sea grass carpeted with oyster shells. Ginger throws herself on the silvery splinters, hail pockmarking her puny body. As she curls into a fetal position, Chris crouches over her in an attitude of consolation or prayer. Actually he is gagging on seawater, but this is the tableau that presents itself to K.

A lightning blast penetrates the room, bringing with it the sour smell of sulfur. The big living room lights up like a stage set, then plunges into darkness as the thunder rolls.

"My God," shrieks Ginger, diving under the sofa cushions.

In minutes, the storm shifts into high. Flashes of lightning blaze onto the frenzied pond. Spray spumes tower against the distant beach. The willows groan, curtsy their pale leaves, flutter upright, shiver down again. The sky, the color of a burned skillet, is poised to pour its contents on the hapless earth.

K. croons over her stricken daughter:

"Higgledy-piggledy,
Ginger and Christopher,
Frightened of lightning and thunder's deep roar.
Quick, babies, come and jump under the coverlets,
Mommy will scare off old Wodin and Thor."

But Ginger only moans in chorus with the circum-navigating wind.

And the rain begins, little silver drops needling into the parsley and the fairy roses until, quickly, it turns into marbled hail whacking the windows. Ginger says, "I need a drink," and, flinging herself out of the cushions, rushes toward the kitchen.

All too soon, the house is a ship aground on the shoals. Its wood frame creaks and shudders, shifts ominously toward the garden. Crouching overhead, the storm seems intent on destroying this monument to artifice in its path. It claws at the windows, hurls a bolt of lightning against the shingles.

K. discovers Ginger under the kitchen table, curled around the chair legs, a bottle of Chivas Regal dead on the tiles next to her. K. crawls under the table too, picks up Ginger's limp hand. Outside, the storm pins inanimate objects to the ground in a cosmic wrestling match.

Dancing in Space

❀ ──────────────── ❀

We're as cozy as a hotdog in the warm bun of humanity. "Can you believe we're here?" Duncan says, giving me a kiss on the ear.

Crosby, Stills and Nash are performing on a stage down the hill, across the valley and up at the top of another hill. With this major sound system, they can harmonize across the miles. As far as I can see, there's a blanket of bodies making out, making up, nursing babies, smoking joints.

"It's been a long time comin' / It's goin' to be a Long Time Gone / And it appears to be a long / Appears to be a long / Appears to be a long time / Yes, a long, long, long, long time / Before the dawn."

Duncan and I scramble to the top of the van and hang on to the sidebars. Mingle with the drifting music.

Duncan touches my breast. "Groovy, babes, we're history."

❀ ────── ❀

This story is about long ago, about yesterday. It was 1969, the end of a decade, the end of an era. The great ones — the Kennedys, Martin Luther King — a memory. Thousands snuffed in Vietnam. Fire and destruction in Detroit and LA. It was getting very late and sad.

But for a lot of us, the lucky ones who could con, cajole, or just vanish from the world to reappear on a pleasant farm in upstate New York in August, the reward would be three incredible days of music and love. Like a bunch of Holy Grailers, we would make our pilgrimage to Woodstock into an encounter with God. Green and hopeful beginnings after a long decade of childhood.

If you were as young as I was then, in the thrall of John and Paul and the Doors, anything else seemed like dog biscuits.

But Time, you thief, put this in. Few of us emerged intact.

I was 14 in 1969, pissed that the decade was disappearing without any help from me. Too young to have been part of the history of peace and love, civil rights, antiwar protests, I listened to stories from my parents. My mother had picketed so many installations in Washington, Chicago, and New York that she didn't seem comfortable without a sign in her hand. "Hey, hey, LBJ, how many kids did you kill today?" "We shall overcome." "Black is Beautiful." "Don't call us girls, call us congresswomen."

Putting the first man on the moon in July sounded like a real bore, only awesome to people like my grandfather, the super patriot. He was Mr. J.T. Warner, of River Road in Manchester, Vermont. The Warners had summered in Manchester since the turn of the century, and Gran was better known around town than the mayor. He hunted with Luke Orvis, fly-fished with the governor, and owned half of Main Street. "Oh, Mr. J.T., I've been holding these books for you," the librarian at the public library simpered, her illegal act rewarded by a benevolent hug and more bucks for the new wing. Gran was not just a big wheel in Manchester, he was the entire Buick Skylark.

I was his favorite grandchild, the city kid he indulged. He wrote to me in early March, "Can't get through the summer without my favorite Fresh Air child. You've got to improve your backhand and learn to dance."

But what I was dreaming of, my fantasies fired by Byron's poetry and a sudden awareness of aging, was the rock concert scheduled for August. That weekend would be everyone's ticket to groove. How could tennis and the ballroom compete? We kids talked of nothing else.

Regrets. I have a few.

The VW bus is painted with butterflies and birds, psychedelic calligraphy, poison green, hot pink, blazing yellow. "Flower Power" and "James Bond is a Virgin."

For three nights Duncan and I have eaten, slept, and made love in the bus, wrapped up in a smelly down bag. It's been beautiful.

Gran would say we were sellouts. I can hear him now. "Sure, those hippies are sincere. Bunch of hypocrites. Take their tactics from Gandhi, their idealism from a philosophy book, and their money from daddy." Then he would amend, "Or grand-daddy."

I will never have the chance to argue with Gran again, though, or try to yell him down. "Gran, you're gross," and he right back with, "I'm trying to smarten you up, cookie, teach you the right way, the American way, you're better off knowing how to change a tire than sitting by the side of the road talking about it." Gran was really the only adult who didn't ignore me.

It was a terrible thing, what I did, and Gran'll never forgive or forget. But I had to make a choice, go up against a tough contender. My mother and father, they'll recover; nothing there that a really good shrink can't cure. Probably ask Gran to pay for the therapy. But Gran, no, he's sure to tell us all to go fish. The worst is, his obsession about the "phony, delinquent left looking for trouble because they're just lazy and bored" will keep growing like that disgusting cancer eating up the monkey's brain in bio lab.

Now Gran will never find out how cool our generation is, how much we're actually waking up the country, changing it, even, because the one person who could stand up to him, maybe change his mind, is dead as far as he's concerned. I wonder if he's watching us on TV — 400,000 of us, all under 30 — spread over 35 acres of a 600-acre dairy farm, listening to Mick and Arlo and Dylan. "Look, world, everything's groovy, peaceful."

Will he be looking for me in the crowd? Or dismissing us all with, "Garbage, nothing but garbage. Human garbage and their man-made kind. Wacked-out flower children sitting in it, walking in it, sleeping on top of it, wall-to-wall bodies in an orgy of irresponsible crap. And for the whole world to watch on television." I must be kidding; Gran's not watching; it would give him a heart attack. In fact, I don't want to think about Gran anymore.

Close to Duncan's van, two people raise a banner. "War is not healthy for children and other living things." Four naked little kids named Dill, Tansy, Kari, and Rama pull at the banner.

The January before that August, I started bugging my parents. They were uptight about me anyway, which I thought was in my favor. Tests showed I wasn't suffering from mono after all, but from a nutritional deficiency causing extreme depression. A brain chemical called serotonin, produced when sugar or starch is eaten, was lacking in my system. The doctor prescribed a diet of carbohydrates and sugar.

As if I would let myself get fat with all that junk. Especially when I was going to be in the history books.

"Everyone's going to Woodstock," I yelled at my mother. "Everyone I know. I have to go, Duncan's invited me."

My mother went on combing her hair, putting me in my place. "You're only 14 years old, way too young to go off on your own with anyone. And to Woodstock! It will be dangerous, drugs, no place to go to the toilet. It's out of the question."

"But Duncan will watch out for me . . ."

"Duncan is 17. And he's a boy. Is he trying to lead you astray?"

My mother could be incredibly dumb, then really scare

you with her psychic powers. I had presented the weekend at Woodstock as a camping trip with music. But my real interest was far more critical: an excursion where I could achieve a major goal, eliminating my technical state of virginity.

"You're just a child," my mother said, staring at my fishnet tights. "You'll grow up fast enough."

"I'm not a child — I could have one, you know," I said, noting with satisfaction my mother turning pale. "And I never get to do anything. Look at you, always in the middle of something exciting."

"You've had your ears pierced," my mother said in her maddening way, doling out her little gifts and promises.

❊ ——————— ❊

Ken Kesey says we're like soldiers in a really successful campaign, but doesn't that sound too much like war? We're just united against the grown-ups, and that definitely includes Gran and my mother and father. Strength in numbers. We're all coexisting in perfect harmony. Like the first time you make love — you'll never forget it.

❊ ——————— ❊

All year, I was immersed in the study of pain. One chapter in my bio textbook especially grabbed me. You cut your finger, nerve endings in the skin are stimulated, causing a pain signal to travel along the nerve to the spinal cord. At the same time, chemicals released in the tissues surrounding the nerve endings also send a pain signal.

When the pain message reaches the spinal cord, chemicals called neurotransmitters are released; these chemicals relay the message to the nerves that will carry it to the brain. Opiates like morphine block the neurotransmitters, lessening the pain signal. But even more important, opiatelike substances produced by the body block the neurotransmitters that relay the pain signals in the brain itself.

Which means that with the right mental attitude you can fend off any kind of distress.

❀ ———————— ❀

At Woodstock there isn't any pain, just lots of grass and a few acid-heads freaking out. A joint costs 25 cents, a hit of LSD $2. But we aren't shooting at each other, we aren't being mean or making each other do what we don't want to do, we're all friends.

❀ ———————— ❀

I wasn't getting along too swift with my family that year. I had two little buttons I wore on my underwear. "Make love, not war" and "Girls say yes to boys who say no." To tease Gran, a widower who still mourned my grandmother, even after 40 years of argument, I wrote him, "If I don't come for the summer, you should join a dating club." And I sent him an ad I had clipped from the *Village Voice.* "Action, action,

action. Meet other members with your interests. Males and females 18 to 70. The modern, fun way to meet. Write Lola, care of the *Voice*."

But Gran had a strong personality, and he ignored my letter. I anticipated a whole lot of pain that summer. I decided to strengthen my pain threshold by biting the inside of my jaw. I couldn't, I wouldn't miss this major event that August would bring, if I had to saw my leg off. I imagined myself in other painful situations. Like in LA when Bobby Kennedy was shot. What I'd do, you know, to capture the shooter? Like leaping onto Sirhan Sirhan the instant the gun appeared? Taking the bullets in my own heart so that we wouldn't all be standing there, staring down at our hero lying still and white on the hotel's kitchen tiles, another martyr dead for his country. I thought about doing that, taking the bullets, and when the next President Kennedy was inaugurated, he would stand over my grave and cry, saying, "Your country thanks you, Jimmie." Or like on that bus with Rosa Parks in Montgomery, Alabama, when she refused to give up her seat to a white man. I know what I would have done. Duncan and I would have delivered a karate chop to the bus driver, while Rosa and the black people cheered. I could smell the police dogs springing at my throat.

❁ ———————— ❁

Far away, like a call to arms, Dylan is singing. I lift my face to Duncan's.

"Got no deeds to do / no promises to keep / I'm dappled

and drowsy and ready to sleep. / Let the morning time drop all its petals on me, / Life, I love you / All is groovy."

Gran's energy had always been at my disposal, because he liked my stubbornness, akin to his, saw me as a worthy opponent and potential ally. To him we were like two fighting fish, so admired for their beauty and guts they would be thrown back to fight again, instead of staring glassy-eyed dead over the fireplace. Gran respected physical people who, he said, coupled inner rhythms with logical minds, enabling them to duke out the wimps. Like the Greeks, he told me, a good American has a sound mind in a sound body.

So, Gran concentrated on me. There was nothing too tough to teach someone who had the will. Instead of my Boston cousins or my cousin Will Parsons right there in Manchester, Gran chose me to teach fly-fishing in the Battenkill, at the bottom of his garden, when my rod was three times my height. He taught me to dive, dove with me into Getta's Hole to prove that no monster lurked below. He started me on tennis lessons when I was six, and in 1967 we won the family mixed doubles championship at the Mountain View Club. I was young enough to preen when we demonstrated our personal best. I also liked being spoiled in return. An ankle bracelet, a trip to Niagara Falls, $50, all came my way courtesy of Mr. J. T., who bragged about his granddaughter all over town. It had been enough, doing good for him, basking in his pride and love.

Recently, family had gotten real old. My mother and

father were locked into their own concerns. Gran had to be my ticket to Woodstock. Somehow, I had to get him to agree. If he did, my mother and father would have to boogie down, stay cool. Gran was the Ultimate Leader, lord of the universe, and my parents, in spite of their denials, were as awed by him as the rest of the world.

As soon as I got off the Manchester bus in June, Gran started agitating about dancing lessons. His other obsession was the July moon landing.

"You and I will see history made together," he said. It was just like Gran to get excited about something as remote as the moon. He might as well be living there, for all he cared about the here and now.

But I threw my arms around his neck. My mind flashed on the pile of Bloomingdale's lacy underwear in my suitcase. I had left my mother in a frenzy. "You don't love me at all; you're only in love with Gloria Steinem," I said spitefully, watching her pin up her blonde hair into a French twist. As soon as I left for Manchester, she was off, too, to picket the Pentagon. "Gran says you women's libbers are too ugly to attract a snake. You hate me because I'm pretty."

My mother said, "Flattery will not get you to Woodstock. But I'll tell you what, I'll buy you a red polka-dot bikini from Garfinkel's. You'll drive 'em nuts in Manchester."

I knew the topic was closed. "And don't disturb your father, either," my mother said. "He's having trouble with the Napalm Movement." My father, a little dark man who played first clarinet for the Philharmonic, had been working for three years on his Tet Overture, and the maestro had been encouraging.

My parents' only appearance in Manchester was a duty

visit every August. I would watch my father and Gran fishing, from my perch on a catalpa tree leaning into the river. "No, no, Stanlee," Gran would say, drawing out my father's name in a contemptuous way, "delicate, delicate. Those trout are smart, they're not your dumb Coney Island bluefish. You gotta tempt 'em. Present the fly to 'em. If you keep stamping around like an elephant, you might as well pack up and go back to Avenue A."

My father, who grew up in Scarsdale, ignored the sarcasm and made his cast, neatly hooking the trees growing along the bank behind him. But he refused to quit. "My sainted Aunt Hannah," he said, using his strongest oath.

"Not too many saints in your religion, are they," Gran said, executing a perfect cast that laid the fly within an inch of the trout. "The trouble with you people is your brains are only agile about book learning . . ." "You people" was the signal. My father would give Gran a hard look, but he would start to cast again. In five years of fly-fishing, he caught three trout. Then he threw them back. But every year, for a week at the end of August, he laid aside his clarinet for Gran's torments.

My parents argued over Gran. "I refuse to fail before that son of a bitch," my father said. "I'll learn to fly-fish if it kills me."

"It won't make him like you any better," said my mother.

"That's a nice thing to say about your own father."

"Why do you care about him?" my mother said. "He's an unapologetic troglodyte."

Gran's disappointment with his sons-in-law was palpable. "It's a mystery to me, Sugar," Gran loved to announce to the girl making our sundaes at Parsons Drugstore. We went there every day for our sugar fix, Gran in his cords and blazer with the diamond lapel flag in his buttonhole. We hoisted ourselves onto the swivel stools and leaned our elbows on the marble counter. Behind us was the card counter, and far from the soda fountain, the Tampax I had just begun to use languished discreetly. I really wanted to get a look at the condoms, but they were kept out of sight under the counter by my Uncle Jasper Parsons, the druggist. The pharmacy smelled of antiseptic and vanilla extract.

"Like I say, it's a mystery," repeated Gran, loud enough for browsing customers to listen in. "Three beautiful daughters, all college girls, smart. And how do they repay me? One of 'em marries a damn Catholic, one a damn Jew, and the other a damn Parsons."

Uncle Jasper, whose forebears had fought with the Green Mountain Boys, stood not three feet away in his pharmacist's cubicle, popping pills into prescription bottles. He sighed at Gran's raving, and kept on counting out tetracycline. Gran's money had bought Parsons Drugstore, and Gran thrived on his daily torture of Uncle Jasper. I wondered when his son, my cousin Will, would cop a package of Trojans to show me.

Even if we weren't listening to the top sixties groups — Baez, Joe Cocker, Country Joe and the Fish, Arlo and his sad face and soft hat telling us we were "forever young," Janis and her hair all wild crying out in pain, "Freedom's just another word for nothing left to lose" — all this would still be an incredible experience.

I run my fingers over Duncan's chest. "Duncan, I can't go back, you know," I say. "To anyone, my folks or to Gran. All summer I was in pain, now they are."

Duncan smiles at me just like Dylan, slow and sweet. He takes another drag.

My head is light, the way it gets when I use up too many carbohydrates on the parallel bars. My chest thumps, and deep down inside, a little spark, like a pilot light on the stove, springs up. Soon it will burst into flame.

"Baby, we're going to be together for a long time."

"You mean after this weekend."

"You bet your bippy."

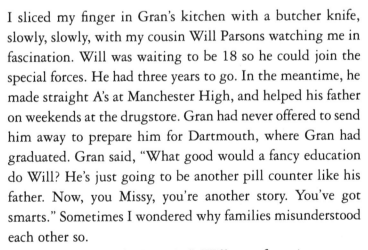

I sliced my finger in Gran's kitchen with a butcher knife, slowly, slowly, with my cousin Will Parsons watching me in fascination. Will was waiting to be 18 so he could join the special forces. He had three years to go. In the meantime, he made straight A's at Manchester High, and helped his father on weekends at the drugstore. Gran had never offered to send him away to prepare him for Dartmouth, where Gran had graduated. Gran said, "What good would a fancy education do Will? He's just going to be another pill counter like his father. Now, you Missy, you're another story. You've got smarts." Sometimes I wondered why families misunderstood each other so.

"That's enough, Jimmie." Will was frowning at me. Blood poured out of my finger, a little river, running down on the chopping block, and dripping to the kitchen floor.

"Quit it, Jimmie," he said. "I'll tell you about the party

I went to at Dover last night." I decided to give up before I severed a nerve. I liked Will's stories about the local commune. "Roger," I said, "Pass me the bandage." I made it tight. There was no pain. I could call up my own neurotransmitter blocks.

"It was really wild, you wouldn't believe it. All these people, little kids, too, using portable potties and making daily garbage runs to the IGA. It looks like they never comb their hair, and while we were sitting around, two guys just turned on with each other's wives right in front of all of us," he said. "Really, they aren't very clean."

I couldn't picture Will fighting the VC, if he worried so much about deodorants. He was sweet, but simple — for instance, he was fascinated to see how long my armpit hair had grown. I hadn't shaved in a year, and I could braid both pits into tiny little plaits. "Did you bring the condoms?" I asked Will. "We could try them out?" I was only teasing, but he blushed and gave me a hickey on my upper arm. Then he reached into his pocket.

❁ ——— ❁

Someone's selling loveburgers for 50 cents, hamburgers in a heart shape. "Get a whole lot," I say to Duncan. "Grass makes me hungry." Duncan climbs down off the van and brings me a pizza. It's tiny. "Be groovy, not greedy," he says.

❁ ——— ❁

Uncle Jasper, Aunt Ellen and Will came to lunch every Sunday. Uncle Jasper and Aunt Ellen took Gran's needling with too much humility. Will was gentle, too, and had a good word for everyone, even Gran's housekeeper, Mrs. Eubanks. He never complained about her disgusting Sunday messes, just stuffed the mashed peas and broccoli au gratin into his socks.

After lunch, Will and I would go down to the river to get away from Gran's hectoring. "Not another cent, Jasper, until you get a better accountant. Only an idiot would permit all those deadbeats you carry on your books."

Will didn't mind that I was Gran's favorite. "Gran isn't mean mean, you know? He's lonely mean." To me, Gran was getting all shriveled up inside, like a nut that had lain too long on the ground.

Will and I took off our clothes, and compared our things. "Your breasts are getting really big," Will said, but he was only being nice. I would have liked him to touch them, to teach me what I needed to know if I was going to Woodstock with Duncan, but Will treated our yearly examination like a lab experiment. I got a lot more excited.

Will's penis was uncircumcised and, to me, with my limited experience, not too big. He was also very blonde down there, like on his head, and I was dark. He laughed and said, "Call it Charlie." I couldn't, however, persuade him to try on a Trojan. Will had some dour sense of propriety that precluded an erection with his cousin, even though I tried my best. And, of course, he was afraid of Gran.

Duncan says we have to let it all hang out, but he means spiritually, because physically, he's shy about letting me look him over. He believes in keeping covered, like the Hare Krishnas, and so far we haven't even been nude bathing in the lake.

❀ —————— ❀

"I know a dark secluded place / Where no one else will know your face . . . ," Gran hummed. Then, "You have a piece of watercress between your teeth." He was leading me skillfully around the dance floor of the Mountain View Club; rather he was skillful, while I tripped and ground my molars. It was the club's annual summer dance, on the Fourth of July.

"Gee, Gran," I complained, "you're totally horrible. And it's hard to follow you. How about we do the monkey or the frug?"

I was embarrassed, not only because I was a dork at the tango, but because I was the only girl at the club dance with a grandfather for a date. As we swept past the gilded floor-to-ceiling mirror that stood behind the bar, I saw a dummy with a painted-on smile. Gran looked handsome, his thick, gray hair topping his tall frame, kept trim and fit from all his exercising.

"Street dancing," he said, digging his bony fingers like knives into my waist, "is for street kids. If you can tango and waltz, you can move in the best circles. Just follow me, slow, slow, quick, quick, slow. That's it, that's better. The Warners have always been good dancers."

He drew me closer to force me to follow him. He had tipped Bill Boggs and his Cumberland Combo to keep playing "Hernando's Hideaway" until I got the idea. I wondered if he could hurt me just a little bit more.

Riding home later, in the big old yellow Buick, Gran said, "See what you can do, Missy? And not with that damn mary ju wannah, either. I read just the other day in the *Burlington Times* that 8 million people have sampled marijuana. You and I are probably the only two people in 100 miles who haven't."

Poor Gran, out of it, as usual. But I *had* learned to do the tango. I listened and I moved, and Gran was out of his mind with happiness. We had won the dance prize, one more win for Mr. J. T. He started off again on "Hernando's Hideaway."

I stared at the interior of the big car. The gear shift was on the wheel and the front seat was as big and comfy as a bed. My father and Uncle Jasper drove little bug cars, where a midget couldn't stretch out.

Gran's Buick reeked of pipe tobacco and Smith's lozenges. I tried biting the inside of my jaw again. Like I was aiming a pistol at a target, I bit down. Harder, harder. Pain exploded in my brain, and I tasted blood. The skin inside my cheek flapped back like an orange peel. I swallowed the blood, and it was sweet, like the lozenges.

"Gran," I said in my most coaxing voice, sliding across the slick, vinyl seat toward him, putting my arm around his shoulders. The cheek hurt like hell. "Will you let me dye my hair purple? You promised me that you'd give me something great if we won the dance contest. Well, I want to dye my hair."

I waited. Gran started to breathe hard, trying to control himself, to be nice as he could on our victorious evening. Then he said, "Don't ruin everything, Missy. Stop trying to be a fool like your folks. Asinine limousine liberals. You learn all this crap about purple hair and tarty dressing from those punks and pansies at that fancy school you go to." He was gearing up.

The Buick slewed from left to right on River Road. "What's happened to this world anyway? It's getting to the point where I like fish better than people. I'd rather be in a trout stream, anyway, where it's between you and the fish, where instincts and skill, not mayhem, win. Sometimes I think you'd be better off living with me, dancing and fishing, enjoying the natural, healthy fruits of life, instead of growing up to be a mad bomber down there in Sodom and Gomorrah."

The Buick slid off the River Road and down toward Gran's house. The old elms and birches along the river swayed in the dark. They were scary. What if Gran insisted I come live with him or be sent to boarding school? He paid for my education, and he dictated the family's economics. I grabbed his hand. "Okay, then, can I go to Woodstock?" Gran slammed the door of the car and left me sitting in the dark.

I'm painting my right eyelid with purple and red flowers. A green leaf and a green stem crawl down my cheek toward my mouth. Duncan likes it. He's stoned. I'm pretty out of it, myself. "Duncan," I say, "you're drunk, D-R-U-N-C-K, drunk."

For the moon shot, Gran prepared as if he were blasting off himself. He felt in his soul that this adventure, Neil Armstrong walking on the moon, would more than offset President Nixon's cowardly withdrawal of 25,000 troops from Vietnam. "It's the work of that Jew Kissinger. Wait till Westmoreland gets here. He'll give that liar Nixon unshirted hell. But the astronauts. They'll make us proud — the Ulysses of space."

Gran even began to babble kindly about dead President Kennedy, because *he* had committed us to land a man on the moon before the decade was out. Otherwise, Gran was of the opinion that the Kennedys and the Reverend King had asked for assassination. "Mindless liberalism," he lectured, "taxing citizens to death for bloody savages who show their gratitude by shooting you down."

But he forgot his retro politics in the excitement of the moment. He had read everything written about space exploration. In his library were books called *Between Earth and Moon, The Space Age,* and *Another Mankind.* He had shelves of H. G. Wells, T. S. Stribling, Lawrence Manning and all these weirdos who wrote about energy rays, fiendish brains, radium-powered zeppelins, moon projectiles carrying dogs and cognac. He was preparing for July 20 as if he and the 600 million other people glued to their TVs were personally supervising the launch.

A week before blast-off, Gran got out his telescope and from accounts in *Scientific American,* calculated the angle for the moon. He kept the TV on day and night, listening to Walter Cronkite blather about the magic of space. "The space race is important, just as the rivalry between Spain and Portugal was in an earlier age." Or, "Many talk about the cost, how our country could use the billions to fight disease and poverty, but it's a goal, without which man's existence would be pointless." Gran could hardly take time out for meals. We ate on trays in the darkened library.

I kept quiet most of the time and watched the TV with Gran. I missed "American Bandstand," but I liked it that Snoopy was the official mascot of the astronauts. Earlier that week, in the "Peanuts" comic, Snoopy went to the moon himself, beating the Americans, the Russians, and the stupid cat next door.

Finally, on July 16, flames and smoke spewed out of the Saturn rocket, and Apollo II lifted off, with a little lunar module named Eagle attached. Gran was right there with the astronauts, flying with them, excited as a space cadet. When Armstrong said, "The Eagle has wings," meaning that the lunar module had broken off from the mother ship and was in orbit around the moon, Gran did a crazy little dance in front of me.

"Oh, boys, oh, boys, beautiful boys. Jimmie, this is something you will tell your grandchildren."

It was all I could do not to dance with him, his excitement was so contagious. But I held back. I figured that what Gran wasn't even considering, would probably reject as subversive, was that Armstrong, Aldrin, and Collins all were facing the possibility of pain and death. They were going off into the scary unknown. The rest of us — mission control, the TV audience, the tourists at the space center, the quick-buck hawkers selling souvenirs — we were gawkers, voyeurs, safe on the ground, while a couple of guys took a *very big* chance. You're all alone when you take chances. Addressing eternity, instead of a trout.

Lying here on the van's top, Duncan's hand making me feel good, I remember Gran humming, "Fly Me to the Moon / And let me play among the stars." He was so out of it. Duncan's hair hangs around his shoulders in a Prince Valiant bob, and he wears a tiny gold earring in his left ear. It doesn't seem possible that before this weekend, our relationship had gone no further than letting him see my underpants.

"The Eagle has landed." Gran and I were together on the couch, eating grapes. I remember them precisely, fat purple Savannahs, seedless and breaking open with a snap as you bit into their juicy insides. Cronkite and space control were screaming. Gran was suffocated with tension, cramped with grapes and anxiety.

In my mind, the TV seemed to be dealing with suicide. Instead of Armstrong climbing down a ladder, clumsy and ridiculous in his space suit, feeling his way onto an alien landscape, I saw him struggling, a noose around his neck, his urgent fingers grabbing at the madness, kicking, kicking. There was a blow-out, then darkness. I tried to concentrate.

Gran said, "Jimmie, look, look." The bottom of the TV screen printed out "10:56 P.M., July 20, 1969". Neil Armstrong was stepping onto the moon. "That's one small step for man, one giant leap for mankind."

"It's a miracle, a miracle, I tell you. All of it, NASA, our country, the greatest on earth; we can put a man on the moon and invent technology so we can all go, too." He was beside himself with joy.

The grape stems lay strewed all around in that dim

library, along with magazines and books and newspapers with pictures of the astronauts, the Sea of Tranquillity, the moon's craters, the lunar module. It was like the two of us were in some dark cave, far from earth ourselves, facing our own uneasy voyage.

I kept my eye on Gran's face. It was white with anxiety and hope. The time had arrived. Gran's world and mine were bound to collide, his dreams of glory and national pride rammed by real life. I put my hand on his leg carefully. On the screen, Armstrong planted a flag on the powdery surface of the bleak moon landscape. Gran seemed to be in a trance. I let my hand move up his leg, and I smiled at him. Just at that moment, Armstrong said to Aldrin, the two of them jumping over moon boulders like kangaroos, "Isn't this fun?"

Gran's eyes were closed. Keep them that way, I prayed, and slowly pulled down the zipper of his fishy blue jeans. The TV flickered, the astronauts staggered along, and we were part of an eerie scene out of my old Buck Rogers comic books. I was gentle. I held my breath, expecting a slap, a push, a horrified look of disgust. In a minute, Gran would run to the phone and book me into a juvenile home. But he didn't. He was slumped on the sofa, his mind far off, on the moon, the stars, the galaxy. He was Captain Nemo, Flash Gordon, Walter Mitty, and Snoopy rolled into one. I slid down the sofa and knelt in front of him.

I was told the moon walk took $2\frac{1}{2}$ hours. At the bottom of the TV screen were printed the words, "Live from the surface of the moon." President Nixon telephoned the astronauts on interplanetary hookup. By 3 A.M., it was over. I only heard about it later; Gran had unplugged the TV and disappeared. But when I woke up on the sofa the next morning, across the room Gran was staring at me, a real old man with glazed eyes and a twitch at the corner of his mouth. I started, "Gran, please Gran, I don't know why . . ." But he interrupted, his voice flat and dry, far away from the Battenkill. "Don't say a word. You've won all right. Just stay out of my sight until you go."

Everybody agrees it was a super love-in. It's raining. The musicians have split; the stage is a soggy mess. The guy who's under the tarp with me, I'm not sure it's Duncan. But who else could it be? I came with him, didn't I? In a little while we're leaving, leaving love and peace and no pain in the rain. Duncan's got to go home; he's got a summer job humping vegetable crates at Hunts Point in the Bronx. He says, "We'll see each other soon, Jimmie, for sure we will." He doesn't say when.

I don't know what I'll be doing. Possibly time. I can't stand the thought of my mom and dad's disappointment, faces screwed up like babies bawling at something they can't understand. Not that Gran will ever tell them the truth. But the school bills and the summer tennis and the fishing are as finished as Armstrong and Aldrin. Can I ever set things right? I doubt it. I don't feel so good, it's like I'm weightless and spinning through a labyrinth of horrible, ugly creatures. And all I'm trying to do is remember how to dance the tango.